Crystal Green lives near Las Vegas, where she writes for the Mills & Boon® Cherish™ and Blaze® lines. She loves to read, overanalyze movies and TV programs, practice yoga and travel when she can. You can read more about her at www.crystal-green.com, where she has a blog and contests. Also, you can follow her on Facebook at www.facebook.com/people/Chris-Marie-Green/1051327765 and Twitter at www.twitter.com/ChrisMarieGreen.

To my fantastic writer buddies, Ann, Ara, Cheryl,
Janet, Judy, Lorelle, Mary and Sylvia.
Eternally onward!

A woman with brown curly hair pulled into a side ponytail that flowed past her shoulder. A lush mouth in an angular face. Light-colored eyes that reflected the same blindsided attraction he was feeling.

All Conn could do was hold his hat to his stomach, which was flipping end over end, crackling with the tremors dancing through it. It was as if a bright light was blazing over his sight, a lightning strike that illuminated that night again.

White sheets on a bed…a woman lying down on them, her hair curled over the pale linen. *Come here, cowboy*, she whispered…

She'd been in St Valentine.

She was the reason he was here. Somehow he knew that without a doubt.

When his vision cleared, she was still staring at him.

Something inside him told him that this had never happened before.

But how could he know for sure?

Dear Reader,

Thank you for returning to St Valentine, Texas, with me!

This time around, you're going to meet Connall Flannigan, a Texas rancher who has returned to town for one reason— after an accident he lost his memory, and he keeps having flashes of St Valentine…as well as a woman. When he finds her, Conn, a former playboy, discovers that he broke her heart.

Not the smoothest start to a courtship, huh?

However, in spite of all his *former* playboy ways, this "new Conn" only knows how he feels about Rita Niles now, and he's got a lot of winning over to do if he's going to regain her affection and trust…

I hope that you'll drop by my website (www.crystal-green. com), where I always have a contest running. I would love it if you'd join me on Twitter, too, at @CrystalGreenMe!

All the best,

Crystal Green

DADDY IN THE MAKING

BY
CRYSTAL GREEN

MILLS
BOON

First published in Great Britain 2013
by Mills & Boon, an imprint of Harlequin (UK) Limited,
Eton House, 18-24 Paradise Road, Richmond, Surrey TW9 1SR

© Chris Marie Green 2012

ISBN: 978 0 263 90079 8
ebook ISBN: 978 1 472 00435 2

23-0113

Harlequin (UK) policy is to use papers that are natural, renewable and recyclable products and made from wood grown in sustainable forests. The logging and manufacturing processes conform to the legal environmental regulations of the country of origin.

Printed and bound in Spain
by Blackprint CPI, Barcelona

Chapter One

"Are you sure you're ready for this?"

Connall Flannigan didn't answer his brother at first. He just kept staring at the three-story, gray-wooded St. Valentine Hotel with its lacy curtains peeking through the windows.

How many times had he seen flashes of this place in what was left of his memory?

As a few obvious tourists brushed by him, Conn looked down at his hand, where he'd been palming a necklace—golden, shiny, with a pendant in the shape of an *R* that separated into two pieces that never seemed to fit together. It'd been found in his pocket after the car accident, and he'd come to St. Valentine to find out why it might've been significant, and to fill the holes in his memory—the gaping spaces from the amnesia.

Conn wrapped his fingers over the necklace. "I'm

not sure about much these days, but this?" He nodded. "I'm sure."

Emmet, who had the same blue eyes and black hair as Conn did under their cowboy hats, looked wary. "I don't know what you think you're gonna find here when the family can tell you everything you need."

Conn shook his head. What he *needed* was something to jar his mind back to where it should be—a place where he would be forced to completely remember just what had happened right before the accident and even previous to that.

A place where he could find himself again.

Once more, the flashes came back to him: this hotel. The name "St. Valentine." A truck bearing down on his pickup just before the world went into a tailspin. And…

He held his breath, waiting for the most puzzling and heart-clutching image of all. *A woman. Dark brown hair, curling over her bare shoulders. Gray eyes full of affection as she looked up at him from where she was lying on the bed, her arms reaching up for him…*

According to Emmet and his other two older brothers, Conn had enjoyed his share of women in the past. He'd never been the type to settle down, they said. Footloose, fancy-free and raising hell whenever possible. One woman on this livestock trip, another on that one.

Yet here he was, in search of this one woman who'd haunted his thoughts since the accident four months ago, flash by provocative flash.

But if there'd been so many women, why her in particular?

And why did he ache every time he thought of her?

"I just want to see what's in here," he said to Emmet,

gesturing toward the hotel. "There's got to be a reason I'm remembering this place more than any other. And a reason I'm recalling…"

"Her," Emmet said just before he chuffed.

Conn sent a sidelong glance to him.

"I've told you," Emmet said. "She's just one of many, Conn. Your time would be better spent on the ranch with your family, relaxing, not running off to a little town that you drove through one night."

"So you've told me." Over and over. Conn's brothers in particular had been pointedly direct with him about his habits—all the flirting, all the disappointed women he'd left behind. They told him that, even though he'd always made it clear that he wasn't in anything for the long haul, he'd always managed to make the ladies think that they were the ones, only to break their hearts in the end.

Conn had a hard time imagining he could be that callous, even if he was friendly enough about loving 'em and leaving 'em.

"Well," Emmet said, planting a booted foot up on the boardwalk. "If that's how you want to go about this, the sooner you get this done, the sooner we can go back home."

Conn grabbed onto the image of home, as if he was afraid of losing that, too. Home was the cattle ranch he ran with his brothers about a hundred miles away from St. Valentine, Texas. They told him that he went on business trips, such as for selling and replenishing livestock—the type of trip he'd been on when he'd had the accident. He'd felt a connection to home when he'd returned there, although there'd been something else, as well, along with the comfort, a yen to go somewhere beyond the ranch. And, months later, it'd turned out to be St. Valentine, for whatever reason.

He stepped onto the boardwalk, taking off his hat and running his fingers through his hair. His heart was beating a mile a minute.

Brown hair...gray eyes...

At the flash that kept coming to him every once in a while, his pulse jerked to a pause before jumping to a start once again.

He was just anxious about getting this over with, getting on with his life. That had to be it.

As he and Emmet walked toward the hotel, then entered the lobby, Conn took a moment to absorb the fringed lamps, the velvet-upholstered furniture, the scent of lemon polish and wood. Tasteful maroon-and-beige wallpaper lent some ease to the tone of the room, but Conn wasn't feeling so easy at all.

They moved to the reception area, where tourists lingered, reading framed newspaper articles on the walls about the so-called ghosts that haunted this Old West establishment—supposedly a gentleman and a lovelorn woman from the 1930s. There would also be articles about the town founder, Tony Amati, and that was why these tourists had come to town on a warm November weekday, Conn thought. They'd been lured by a new mystery that had been uncovered by a couple of town reporters who'd realized that old Tony, the former Texas Ranger, had died under a shroud of seeming conspiracy and strange circumstances.

To hear the tales, Amati, who'd settled in these parts and founded St. Valentine way back in the late 1920s, had started to matter more than ever around here after a man who was his spitting image had wandered into town over four months ago, before Conn had arrived. People had started looking very closely at the pictures of the town founder then, comparing them to the stranger, the cryptic Jared Colton. They'd started getting very interested in Tony, too—a man who'd done so much for St. Valentine, yet had managed to remain a puzzle all the same.

Both Tony and this modern-day stranger had certainly captured everyone's romantic inclinations and imagination. And the town, which had suffered through rough economic times, was now starting to benefit from the story, attracting more and more tourists. Just how had Tony died? everyone wondered. And *why* had he been so darn reclusive? Everyone wanted to poke around and solve the mysteries. Magazine articles and travel shows had been sniffing around town, too—there'd even been some kind of TV ghost show that had camped out in the St. Valentine Hotel, the papers said.

Yup, Conn had sure done all the research he could about St. Valentine before coming out here. Not that it had helped with his *own* mysteries.

"Any of it look familiar?" Emmet asked.

"Not really."

Emmet gestured toward the reception desk. "You want to find out if you checked in here that night?"

The hotel had wanted to see some ID in person before giving out that kind of sensitive information. "Yeah."

Conn took a step toward the long desk, then stopped in his tracks, stilled by a bolt of electricity.

A woman with brown curly hair pulled into a side ponytail that flowed past her shoulder, her torso covered by a white old-fashioned, high-collared blouse that was obviously a part of the hotel's uniform. She had a lush mouth in an angular face, and light-colored eyes that reflected the same blindsided attraction he was feeling.

All Conn could do was hold his hat to his stomach, which was flipping end over end, crackling with the tremors dancing through it. It was as if a bright light was blazing over his sight, a lightning strike that illuminated *that* night again.

White sheets on a bed...a woman lying down on them, her hair curled over the pale linen. "Come here, cowboy," she whispered...

She'd been in St. Valentine.

She was the reason he was here. Somehow, he knew that without a doubt.

When his vision cleared, she was still staring at him, just as if she'd seen one of the ghosts that this hotel was supposed to house.

Did his knees ever go this weak with all those other women he'd supposedly been with? It sure as hell hadn't happened with the nurses at the hospital. Then again, they hadn't looked like this brunette.

Besides, something inside him told him that this had *never* happened before.

But how could he know for sure?

Clutching the necklace until its edges dug into his palm, Conn left Emmet and went to the desk. The woman was still behind it, by herself, but from the way she looked away from him, down at the counter, Conn could tell that she wished she had any guest but him in line for some service.

In fact, as she glanced up again, her gaze had gone from thunderstruck to steely, all in a tumultuous second.

He didn't even have the chance to utter a hello before she said in a low tone, "So you're back."

Steely, all right. A gritted comment that nearly set him back on his heels.

This *was* the woman in his fragmented memories, right? The limpid-eyed lady who'd begun to appear to him recently at night, giving him pleasant dreams. The one who'd been so happy to be in his bed.

He showed her the necklace, the *R* split in half across his palm. She sucked in a breath, but then, as if she was real good at recovering quickly, that breath turned into a small laugh.

"You came here to return *this?*" She was still talking quietly enough so that her voice didn't carry. "Better late than never, I suppose."

Return it? Why had he taken it in the first place? He thought that maybe he should apologize about something, but he wasn't sure just what it was he would be sorry for.

"Can we talk?" he asked. "I need—"

"Talk? That's a good euphemism." She laughed again, taking up a pile of paper and neatly straightening it on the desk. "I'll tell you what, cowboy—you just keep that trophy of yours and we'll call it even." She nodded at the necklace he was still holding. "You've had it for going on four months, anyway."

Four months. She would've been here, at the St. Valentine Hotel, during his fateful trip.

He glanced down at the necklace again. The letter *R*. Then he looked up at her name tag.

Rita.

Except, on the tag, her name in cursive was one continuous string, unlike the separated necklace. Unlike his life now.

She called over a young clerk who was straightening a rack of brochures, and once she was manning the desk, Rita walked to the far end of the structure, to a quiet corner where the desk still barred her from him. Conn could hear Emmet clearing his throat as he left him behind.

Conn peered over his shoulder at his brother, who was awkwardly standing there with a "So? What gives?" expression. But it might've also been a "Told you this woman was just as temporary as the others" look.

Conn jerked his chin toward Rita, conveying that he still had a lot to take care of and that maybe Emmet should read some of those framed articles on the wall to pass the time. Emmet shrugged and wandered off.

As Rita shuffled papers, probably wishing Conn would think she was too busy to continue talking, he didn't take her none-too-subtle hint.

"I apologize for the inconvenience," he said softly, not wanting to make a scene. Strangely, that woman-luring charm his brothers had commented on still came easily to him when not much else did. "But I could really use your help."

He added a smile for good measure. He had a feeling it had worked a million times.

"My help?" She didn't look up at him. "Are you asking me for a place to stay the night again? A warm bed? A willing woman who doesn't know any better than to listen to your promises?"

Oops.

"Begging your pardon," he said, "but I hope you'll believe me when I tell you that I don't know *anything* I said to you that night. There's a good reason I came back here, and it wasn't to return a necklace."

Eyes narrowed, she waited for him to go on.

He leaned his elbow on the desk, setting his hat down on it. Even from this distance, she smelled like berries and vanilla, and he nearly closed his eyes as the scent traveled through him, warming him deep down. It was as if he hadn't ever forgotten this part of her, even though the memory had just reemerged.

But he shook himself out of it. Good God, he didn't have time to be sniffing around a random woman who was no doubt one of many more. He needed to talk to her, not to get her into bed again.

"This is going to sound odd," he said. How did a guy get around to telling a woman something that amounted to the lamest excuse in the world? Why would she even believe him?

But what else was he going to say?

He was still holding her necklace. "I'd really like your help in… Well, first off, I need to know when we…"

"Did it? You've got to be kidding me."

All right. That was one way of getting over the awkwardness. She was just as forthright as his brothers.

"I wish I were kidding," he said. "I had some business at the Hervy Ranch about a half hour away in July—"

"I know. You were dealing with livestock. You told me that right before you talked me into…"

She pressed her lips together, color rising in her cheeks. A buzz skimmed his belly at just the mention of what had gone on between them, even though this wasn't the time or place for it.

The important thing was that he'd done more than just had sex with her. She was someone he'd *talked* to around the time of his accident, although he didn't know how long they had chatted before getting to the bedroom. If she could just give him more details about their time together, maybe that would kick-start his brain and he could piece together more of what had happened before and just after the accident.

She shot him a slanted look. "Why the hell wouldn't you know when we…" She lowered her voice, glancing around. Discovering that the lobby had emptied, she added, "Were together?"

Here it went.

"When I left St. Valentine," he said, "I got in an accident on the way to my appointment. Enough of one to send me in an ambulance to the hospital."

She raised her eyebrows. On her face he saw shock… until her gaze softened for a vulnerable moment.

"An accident?" she asked.

"That's right. And afterward I didn't remember where I was, who I was… My brothers and mom were there to help me put things together. Most things, anyway. I've got holes right where a lot of my memory used to be."

She just kept watching him, her gaze finally going from soft and gray to unreadable and cool.

Then she laughed softly, and it wasn't a funny laugh. Her gaze was sad now.

"This *is* a joke, right?" she asked.

"No." What kind of psychotic would approach her again just to lay a line like this on her?

"Whatever it is, it's not funny at all."

Conn started to assure her that he was deadly serious, but she had already abandoned her stack of papers and rounded the desk corner, her body fully revealed now.

As he laid eyes on her slightly swelling stomach pressing against her skirt, he froze, unable to follow her.

Rita Niles never looked back at him. She just blindly headed for the hallway, then the closed door to the tea-room, hoping he wouldn't see where she'd gone.

Conn Flannigan, the man she'd put so much hope in, even after one night. Dumbly, naively, regretfully.

She calmly opened the door, but as soon as she was in the empty kitchen, she leaned on a stainless-steel counter, dizzy, her pulse so loud in her ears, so wild in her chest, that she almost slumped to the floor.

But not quite, because she'd promised herself that nobody was ever going to do this to her again. Not after what her ex-fiancé, Kevin, had done to her. And definitely not after she'd dropped her guard during a wonderful night of seduction with this cowboy, finally believing that she'd been wrong about love all these years.

She rubbed the curve of her belly, fighting the tears.

Conn Flannigan.

When she'd seen him in the lobby today, it'd shocked her right down to her toes, her body tingling in places that should've been smart enough to go numb after she thought she'd been left high and dry by him. But, with him standing there, with his thick, black hair that curled up at the ends, with his shining blue eyes, with every inch of lean, tall cowboy in a Western shirt, jeans and boots, she'd come alive in very dangerous ways.

And it was happening now, too, as that night filtered back to her.

She'd been sitting in the Queen of Hearts Saloon, re-signed to hours of drudge work ahead of her at the hotel.

She'd been in threadbare jeans, an untucked blouse, with her hair pulled back in a haphazard ponytail, yet when he'd walked in, she was the only one he'd looked at.

And that look… Even now, she shivered from the intensity of what it'd done to her—breathing fire under and over her skin, sizzling through her until it consumed every inch. She could've even sworn that time had stopped for both of them, could've sworn that every one of his cells was vibrating just as hard as hers were.

If she had the capacity to believe in love at first sight, she might have said that she fell in love with him then and there. Maybe, in those first few crazy moments she'd gotten the closest to love she would ever get again.

He'd ambled right over, offering to buy Rita dinner, sweet-talking her until her knees went to jelly. She'd never clicked so quickly with anyone, flirted so easily, not even with Kevin, who'd taken the slow route with her during days of high school dances and after-graduation dates. But Conn?

That night—that damned magic night—it'd felt as if Conn had been the man she should've held out for all along.

He'd walked her back to the hotel, and much to her surprise, she'd found herself forgetting every lesson she'd learned. Her body overtaking her mind, she'd invited him in, first to the lobby. Then, when she'd resigned herself to ditching her all-night work shift, she'd clandestinely invited him to an empty room a floor below her own quarters in the hotel.

She'd been lost in him so deeply that she'd thought…

Well, she'd thought that things could be different this time. Thought that she'd somehow wonderfully crossed a line she'd drawn years ago after Kevin had left her and their daughter.

It'd been that good with Conn, and that was why she hated him—because he'd seemed to be the answer for her. Because he'd made her body and soul agonize for so many nights afterward.

Now, Rita rested her hand on the baby growing inside of her. Ridiculous. She'd been ridiculous to think that one night might change everything, especially for a person who'd spent a long while shuttering herself away, slat by slat, until she looked at the world only through the cracks.

But...

For one night, it really had been that good.

He hadn't checked in to the hotel, so she'd never gotten his contact information. Besides, he'd told her he was going to be back, so she hadn't asked for a phone number, an address. He'd taken her necklace in a playful moment, saying he would return it to her that night when he returned for more, almost as if it were a vow.

She'd believed in him.

Believed and been abandoned.

But, she thought, he'd had *amnesia*.

She started to laugh—a crazy, cracked-at-the-edges laugh that trailed into the threat of more tears as she leaned her head down on her arms, which still rested on the kitchen counter.

Amnesia. How stupid did he think she was?

As she stifled another sob, doubt crept into her. What if...

No. Amnesia was so far out of the question that she *shouldn't* believe it.

Still, the doubts stayed with her, even as she heard

footsteps outside the kitchen door. She put on her "boss face," straightening up, swiping at her cheeks and finding a few stray tears, then walked toward the entrance to the tea room, just as Margery Wilmore busted through the hallway door.

She had a plump chest and was motherly and gray-haired. "How's my Rita doing?"

"Right as rain." Rita glanced at her watch. "Tea prep already?"

"Like clockwork." The older woman sent Rita a concerned look. "You okay, honey?"

Rita nodded. Margery was a carryover from the days when Rita's mom used to run the hotel, back before she and Dad had passed on. When Rita had taken over at the age of twenty-three, Margery had "kindly" tried to offer all kinds of advice, even though Rita had been working at the hotel since she was old enough to carry out orders, raised to take over operations one day. Now, ten years later, Margery still hovered, casting a suspicious eye at Rita's tummy when she'd started showing recently.

But didn't everyone hover in their own ways? After Kevin, Rita had sort of become St. Valentine's pet project. The town screwup who'd been saving up to go to college for years after graduation—and wouldn't you know it? She'd actually earned a business scholarship but had given it up when she'd gotten preggers.

A pregnancy had been out of character for her, the straight-A student. And, even more off-putting to a lot of folks around here, after Kevin had left her and she had proudly set out to be a single parent, she had refused interference or unwanted advice from everyone who "knew better" in a town where traditional family values ruled.

Now, she was going for another round of out-of-wedlock parenthood.

"You're running yourself ragged," Margery said, resting a hand on Rita's cheek to test her temperature.

Rita deftly shied away. "I'm just fine."

The older woman clucked her tongue. "You and your stubbornness. Someday it's all going to catch up to you, especially raising Kristy alone."

That's right—Margery knew best. How could Rita have forgotten?

Her cell phone rang, and gratefully, she went into the empty hallway and answered, not caring who was on the other end. When she heard the voice of her best friend, Violet, she almost cheered.

Too bad Vi's actual words didn't have the same effect on her.

"Is it true?" she asked.

Rita wouldn't play dumb. "You already heard?"

"Small town. Grapevine. Newspaper reporter. Go figure."

Gossip traveled at the speed of light in St. Valentine, but it wasn't as if Rita had never been its subject before.

"He just showed up, Vi. Out of nowhere."

"Want to talk about it over some lunch?"

They agreed to meet in ten minutes at the Queen of Hearts Saloon, which belonged to Vi's family. Rita went to the lobby, taking care to scan it before she entered.

No sign of the cowboy.

Relieved—was that the word she was looking for?—she crossed the lobby, telling her desk clerk that she was going on lunch break, then feeling the girl's eyes on her. And why not, when Janelle had probably seen Conn Flannigan in here with the necklace and heard some of their conversation while she'd been straightening the brochures?

Head held high, Rita tried her best not to feel like the town screwup once again as she left the hotel, wondering if Conn Flannigan was outside.

Wondering if she was going to be able to avoid telling him just who the father of her unborn baby was.

Chapter Two

"I wish he'd just stayed away," Rita told Vi as she sat across from her at the Queen of Hearts in an out-of-the-way corner booth where the low-volume country songs on the jukebox were even more muted. The wagon wheel light fixtures hovered overhead, and a bunch of regulars ate burgers and drank beer at the bar, surrounded by sepia-hued pictures of the town during its early days.

"It sounds to me like he really does have amnesia." Vi's brown eyes reflected sympathy. Even though she was on lunch break from the small-town-reporter's desk, she had an iPad next to her, ready to catch any breaking news should it come their way. "It'd be a good reason for him to come back here, retracing his steps before his accident. And he'd have no idea how ticked off you'd be. Besides, who goes around telling stories like that unless they're true?"

Rita hadn't touched her chef's salad yet, but Vi was munching away on her fries. She'd been there for the morning after when Rita had still been on cloud nine after her night with Conn. But Vi had also seen the aftermath and how it'd decimated a newfound confidence for Rita that had lasted less than twenty-four hours before she'd felt the shame of supposedly being lied to and left behind once again.

"So what're you going to do?" Vi asked, dipping a fry in catsup.

"What can I do?" Rita jabbed at a piece of ham with her fork. "I shouldn't have *done* anything in the first place—except for running straight out of here when he bellied up to my table that night. I should've known—"

"Hey, you couldn't have known." As Vi leaned forward to rest a hand over Rita's free one, her shoulder-length, dark red hair swung forward. "You were ready to move on after years of hating yourself for what happened with Kevin."

"You weren't happy when I told you about Conn after our…night."

"I was being protective. But now there's a baby involved, and that changes everything."

Rita cradled her slightly curved tummy with her free hand. "That night, I should've just thought more about what it felt like when Kevin left. *That* would've stopped me from giving in to Conn."

But she hadn't been able to think about anything or anyone…except for the cowboy at her table, his eyes sparkling with fun, drawing her into their depths with "why not?" allure.

But, as she'd waited for him the day and night afterward, she'd found out "why not." The minutes had ticked by to one hour…two…then to midnight. And still no Conn. The next morning had come, then passed, then the next and the next.

By that time, she knew she'd been had, and she'd closed up her heart tighter than ever, knowing that she was the only one she could depend on.

And then she'd missed her period, although Rita couldn't and wouldn't regret getting pregnant.

Maybe that was what life had in store for her. Always a great mother to the children she loved more than anything, but never a wife.

"You know what the most embarrassing part is?" Rita finally asked.

Violet swallowed her bite of burger. "What?"

A wounded laugh escaped. "There was something that kept needling at me, telling me that there was a really good reason he didn't come back."

"And there ended up *being* a good reason. Doesn't it make you feel better to know that he didn't reject you? That it had everything to do with circumstances beyond his control?"

Vi was wearing one of those looks filled with optimism. And why shouldn't she? This weekend, she was going to marry millionaire Davis Jackson, her star-crossed lover from high school. They had been run through the gauntlet after Vi had come back to town after having lost her job on a city newspaper and returned to St. Valentine to lick her wounds. Davis had always loved her—the girl from the wrong side of the tracks—but Vi hadn't been sure he was pursuing her again because of that or to get payback for how she had broken his heart. Now, though, everything was wedding marches and roses for her.

No, Rita didn't feel nearly as positive as Vi.

"I'm just considering myself lucky to have escaped this one," she said. "Conn is my cautionary tale."

"For what could happen if you should ever let your guard down again and someone crushes you for real. I get it, Rita."

"I mean, he didn't return to St. Valentine to request my forgiveness or to sweep me off my feet again, right? And if he saw my stomach, he probably flipped."

"You don't *know* if he saw it?"

"I didn't look at him to make sure while I was high-tailing it out of the lobby."

"You couldn't bring yourself to see his reaction. I get that, too." Vi sighed. "But if you left him in the dust like that, how can you be so sure just what he wants to do?"

What he wanted to do... A glimmer of the same excitement she'd felt that night—and even today when she'd first seen him—shimmered deep in Rita's chest, where it felt as if something were struggling to come alive.

Why wouldn't it just go away?

Vi leaned back in her seat, probably knowing Rita wouldn't answer the rhetorical question. "Word has it that there was something in the air when you two laid eyes on each other this afternoon, you know."

What did everyone else know? "And since when are you such a fan of gossip?"

Vi made a "touché" gesture. She'd suffered plenty of gossip herself, when her off-limits millionaire had flown in the face of everyone in town to court her.

A waitress came by, asking if they would like anything else. Rita requested a to-go container and the server left without dropping off a check. She knew Vi had it covered, since her parents owned the place, which had seen a spike in customers since Vi's journalistic work had been featured in a "Tony Amati Mystery" story that had gotten some airtime on a national news magazine program last month. It was true that Vi and Davis, who owned the small-town newspaper, hadn't been able to dig up much information about Tony lately, but that hadn't stopped them from staying the course.

"To-go?" Vi asked. "You're deserting me?"

"I'll have to eat the rest after I pick up Kristy from preschool. She likes the little chunks of ham, anyway."

Vi wasn't letting this go. "So…that's going to be it, then? You're going back to the hotel, back to the bubble of your reception desk?"

"Safest place on earth."

"Rita…"

She slumped in her seat. "Listen, I know that you've fallen in love and you just want everyone else to be as happy as you are. But I can't do it again. I can't have my pride and…" She rested a hand over her heart. "I can't have it bruised again." Then she put her hand on her tummy, rubbing it. "So, yes, I'm going back to the hotel to do some maintenance work after I pick up Kristy. And I'm going to hope that Conn Flannigan has already driven back home without knowing anything more than he needs to."

Then she eased toward the edge of her booth seat, intending to get out. "The bottom line is that he doesn't really remember what went on between us that night. That's probably a blessing in disguise. I'm sure we both acted in a way we'd regret now, after the heat of the moment."

"If that's how you want it."

Great—the guilt trip. But Rita was firm in her resolutions. That night four months ago, she'd rushed into something she'd never thought she would be going into again. But now, with some time and distance behind her, she really did think that she'd dodged a bullet. The hotel had been busier than ever, and Kristy needed a mother who was focused on her, not on hormonal desires and scatterbrained affairs.

"Rita?" Vi smiled sadly. "I'd give anything to see you and the kids happy."

"All of us are just fine. We'll be very happy."

Rita just wanted to raise her daughter and this new child to be more than what *she'd* been known as in St. Valentine ever since Kevin had become a bitter, different man, then left her for the other woman she'd found out he'd been seeing while she was pregnant.

Yes, Rita was the hard-luck case. But she'd done a damned good job of raising Kristy in spite of that until—

No, she didn't want to mull over Conn Flannigan again. Didn't want her heart to ache with an agonizing heat just at the thought of him.

The waitress brought the to-go container, and Vi stayed seated as Rita grabbed her purse, sliding the strap over her shoulder.

"Someday," Vi said, "you're not going to be able to ignore how you feel, Rita. You found it real easy to fall in love when we were kids. I wish it could be just as easy for you nowadays."

Rita's pulse thudded in bruised rhythm, but just as

she was about to buck up, the room suddenly went still, as if something had entered and caught everyone's attention.

When Rita glanced toward the entrance, her throat was tight. Was it…?

Then she saw who had come in, and she relaxed, even though her heart jittered in her chest.

It wasn't Conn, thank goodness. But it *was* a man in beaten jeans and a long-sleeved black Western shirt who had taken a seat at a table that was removed from everyone else. He left his black cowboy hat on, the better to shade a dark-eyed, stoic face that everyone in town hadn't stopped talking about since he'd arrived months ago, only to settle just on the outskirts of town after getting a job on a nearby ranch and renting a cabin.

The Tony Amati look-alike—Jared Colton. And he was just as aloof as he'd been when he'd first arrived. He was a ringer for all the photos of Tony Amati hanging on the hotel and Queen of Hearts walls, and even though everyone had their own theories about how he was connected to the town founder, he was still a mystery that Vi and Davis had been trying to solve through their journalistic investigation and the published articles that had been picked up by some national outlets.

Rita didn't mind him at all, seeing as he'd helped stir up interest in St. Valentine, which had been languishing after the kaolin mine had stopped producing "china clay" for things such as plastic, paints and paper. Jared and Tony had certainly pumped up tourism and given her more to do, so that she could forget about her cowboy.

"The cipher cometh," Vi whispered across the table.

She grabbed her iPad with one hand, polishing off the last fry on her plate with the other. "I've got work to do."

"He's already told you a million times—no interviews."

"Maybe this is the time he'll break." Vi flashed her a determined smile and was off.

Jared saw her coming, but his expression never altered, even as Vi took a seat across from him.

When Rita left the saloon, she was careful to look both ways on the boardwalk before fully coming outside. Not seeing Conn Flannigan anywhere, she started to walk toward Kristy's preschool, telling herself that Conn had gone home again.

But why didn't it feel so great to realize that?

Conn and Emmet had stopped at a little Tomorrowland-like joint called the Orbit Diner for lunch, and now they were walking back to Emmet's pickup truck, which they'd parked just off Amati Street, nearer to the hotel.

"I wish you'd reconsider," Emmet said.

"There's too much to walk away from here." During lunch, Conn hadn't said anything about the tiny pooch of Rita's belly. For all he knew, it could've been due to a weight gain, but he planned to get to the bottom of the story today.

His pulse gathered speed every time he thought of her coming out from behind the hotel desk…the little bump on her…the way she'd left him frozen in his tracks.

What if she *was* pregnant?

Something—a memory?—stirred in the back of his mind, but it didn't come through. Not yet. All he could hold on to now was his confusion at not knowing what the hell he felt.

A baby, he thought.

Was he even the type of guy who would make a good father?

A tiny sense of panic ran through him, icing any emotion, as he and Emmet passed one of the burros that roamed St. Valentine. The critters were ancestors of the first burros that'd been used in the mines, and they were a tourist draw now, a town characteristic just as quirky as the Indian jewelry shop, the Old West trimmings or the mercantile that still made taffy and sold clothing, kitchen goods and souvenirs.

Emmet hung his thumbs in his belt loops while they walked. "Conn, I'm really not comfortable taking the truck and stranding you here."

"Why? There's a rental car office in the new part of town up the hill. There're clothes stores, a pharmacy and even a real live doctor, just in case you think I'll need one." He'd brought his meds, too, but he doubted he was going to stay long enough for them to run out.

"Maybe we should both check into rooms."

"Maybe you should just get back to the ranch. They can't afford to have both of us gone."

Just as he finished, the words died in the air, because straight up ahead, on the boardwalk, there she was.

Rita, in her old-fashioned hotel uniform—the blouse and knee-length skirt. Her legs were long, especially in the light black stockings that clung to the curves of her calves. She was shapely all over, not slender, but...

His hands skimming her hips...waist...the sides of her breasts...

Desire flushed through him like a flood of lava.

Every time he saw her he remembered yet another sensual moment. What else would come to him, though? Enough solid details to get him on his way to the rest of his life?

Emmet sighed, then said, "Call me when you're done and we'll get that rental car."

"Will do."

Rita was heading the other way, her back to him now. As he walked at a steady pace to catch up, his gaze couldn't help but caress her rear end, which was cupped by that modest, yet somehow sexy, black skirt.

It was as if she sensed him before he said a word. Or maybe she just heard his boot steps on the boardwalk.

As she stopped and looked at him, those gray eyes were wide again. Something exploded in his chest as their gazes locked, and his pulse jumped, skipping over the next beat and landing hard on the other side.

Was he wrong, or did it seem as if she was just as rocked?

She started walking again, as if she was either resigned that he would continue to hound her or she was intent on just getting away.

"Aren't you gone yet?" she asked, training her eyes straight ahead.

He laughed at her gumption. Somehow, laughter felt natural with her, as if they'd done a lot of it that night, even if there wasn't much in store now. "I think there's more in St. Valentine for me besides sightseeing."

They were passing her hotel. Outside, where rusted iron benches waited like timeless sentries, a flock of geriatric men and one silver-haired woman wearing an Indian blanket around her shoulders were smoking cigars and watching the world go by. That included Rita and Conn, too, and their gazes followed them, even after Rita nodded a greeting.

Conn thought that she looked a little proud, her chin lifted slightly, as if she was daring someone to say something about her weight gain or…

The baby.

Again, his heart raced. He had to ask. It was just a matter of when.

She spoke when they were far enough away from the crowd. "I remember you were just as persistent then as you are now."

"My brothers and mom call it 'willfulness.' They say I decide on something and I stick to it."

"Yet you don't remember that about yourself."

"No, but it seems to be something I didn't lose in that accident."

She didn't respond, so he decided he would do more talking. "One of the first things they said to me when I was recovering is that I'm a true cowboy, a man who's at home on the range more than anyplace else. They say I'd rather be there than off the ranch in pursuit of a real life."

"I know what you mean."

He got the feeling that Rita had heard this about herself, too, except in her life, it was all about the hotel, not a ranch.

Strange that he would think this, though. Had she told him something similar that night?

Was it starting to come back to him now?

He reached inside his head but couldn't recall it. All he could grasp were faraway things like sitting alone on his cabin porch, listening to the night sounds on his swing, enjoying what he had as a bachelor, content with nothing more.

Rita gave him a sidelong glance as they kept walking. It was now or never.

He took off his hat, holding it in his hands. "I couldn't help but notice…"

He motioned toward her stomach, trying to avoid the indelicacy of the words.

Immediately, she placed her palm there, as if protecting herself. Was she going to tell him to go to hell for saying she'd put on some pounds? Or…

Then she began walking again. "Don't worry about it. The baby isn't yours."

Was that relief sliding through him, from chest to toe?

"I only wanted to make sure," he said. "I might not know much about myself, but I do know that if it came down to it, I wouldn't have left you in a lurch."

"A baby's not a lurch."

Damn, she was making him work hard. "I didn't mean it that way. I'm sorry, Rita."

She stopped walking again, her hands on her hips as she shook her head. "You've been sorry a hundred times already."

"Listen, all I want to know is—"

"I know what you want to know and I get the feeling that you won't be going anywhere until you drag it out of me."

Did she actually believe him now when he said that he had amnesia?

"So you just want me to paint you a picture of a memory, is that all?" she said, seemingly giving in.

"You want me to fill in what happened before your accident?"

"I'd be grateful for it." He held his hat with both hands. "I've had snippets of memory, where nothing has made much sense. So I thought I'd come back here, based on a few flashes, to get my past straightened out."

She smoothed down her skirt, as civil as could be. "There's really not much to tell. It started when you strolled into the saloon down the street while I was grabbing dinner."

A slight glow lit in her eyes before she quickly banished it. Was she thinking of how it'd been, with him walking into the room, latching gazes with her?

A bang-up attraction just like the one he was feeling now?

Was she feeling it, too, but doing her damnedest to tamp it down?

"I was taking a break from doing some repair work in the hotel," she said. "So it was going to be a long night. I own the place, along with my brother and sister, but I'm the one who runs it. And the only time I have to do catch-up work is when the desk isn't very busy. But it's been that way ever since the Tony Amati story came to the forefront."

"I heard all about that."

She crossed her arms over her chest, as if resisting any small talk. "Anyway, you came right over to my table. Charming. *Persistent.* Long story short, we ended up in bed in one of the empty hotel rooms. And when you left the next morning, you said you'd…"

He'd already guessed what he'd said, and he wondered how many women he'd done it to and if he'd really meant it at the time.

"I told you I'd be back," he said.

"Yes. You said you'd come back after you'd taken care of your business for the day." She fingered her collar, as if missing the jewelry she used to wear. "You took my necklace from my pile of clothing and said you wanted to bring it with you. You were in a playful, good mood. 'It's just some insurance,' you said. 'A guarantee I'll come strolling through the lobby again tonight.'"

Insurance? A guarantee? Okay, from what he remembered about himself, this didn't sound like him at all.

Had he been toying with her? His brothers—his best friends—had told him that he was a pretty harmless scamp, but it didn't sound like it right now.

Why hadn't he just made it clear to her that their one-night stand was merely that?

A sense of bewilderment rotated within him, as if trying to find a place to stop, to lock in and provide some clarity, but it never did.

"At any rate," she said, still cool, "that's the gist of it."

He wanted to ask her just when she'd stopped expecting him to come back, but he wasn't sure why he was even wondering.

She started walking again, and he knew she'd said all she was going to say. He knew that he'd done a real number on her, too, whether she showed it or not.

"I'm sorry," he said again, following her, taking the necklace out of his back pocket and holding it out. "I wish I could—"

"You don't have to wish anything." She ignored the necklace. "Actually, it's good to know the reason you didn't come back—not to say I'm glad you were in an accident, but…" She blew out a breath. "At least you're okay."

He acknowledged that, nodding, then out of pure impulse, took her hand, intending to put the necklace in it. She gasped just as a zing of energy flew up his fingers, his arm—

Holding her… Curves against his palms, sleek, smooth, so beautiful…

He came out of it as she pulled her hand away from his and walked off again.

"You can keep it. It's only a bauble."

But, as he stood there, he got the feeling that this necklace—and everything that went along with it—no doubt meant a lot more than that to her.

He wanted to apologize again, but by now, apologies were just air. Meaningless.

He caught up with her in a couple of long strides. "If there's anything else you can tell me—"

The words spilled out of her, as if the sooner she said them, the sooner he would leave. "You said that two out of three of your brothers are happily married. They tease you about being a bachelor until you'd like to punch their lights out. Your mom's a widow, and you think that, more than anyone, she wishes you'd get out more to find someone who'd make your days 'shine all the brighter,' as she'd say. That's what happened to her and your father—true, fast love."

What? "I told you all that?"

"Well, we didn't sleep much, whether it was talking or…" She trailed off, as if she regretted how far she'd gone in this conversation.

But he was swamped by yet another image. *Holding her against him as she closed her eyes, pressing kisses to her eyelids, one by one, then the tip of her nose. Watching her in the glow of a soft lamp as she drifted off to sleep. Feeling something unfamiliar twisting inside of him, as if being born...*

But wasn't he the ultimate cowboy bachelor?

The same twisting sensation ripped through him now, as if daring him to define what it was.

Up ahead, he could hear children's laughter, the clang of a playground, past all the dust-brushed Old West buildings. Rita kept leading him toward it.

"Rita," he said, "when I came back here, it was because of you."

This time, when she slowed down, she almost seemed to stumble before she straightened her posture. "What?"

"I had this fragment of a memory..." He gentled his tone. "About you. It drove me to find you, even if I can't remember exactly why. I keep thinking that if I spend some time with you, it's going to shake things loose in my head."

His directness had apparently stunned her, because she kept walking slowly, not looking at him.

But then, she did sneak a glance, her expression even more torn now.

He'd played his last card with her.

They stopped at a chain-link fence that separated them from swing sets, a teeter-totter and a field where children were playing tag and doing somersaults and cartwheels in front of a woman wearing a floppy camp hat. Next to the field stood a small pastel-colored building with a mural on it. In the mural, children of all sizes and colors laughed, held hands and peered up at a rainbow.

One little girl with dark curls just like Rita's spied her, and she jumped up, then waved.

Rita waved back as the girl picked up a bag from the edge of the grass and came running toward a swinging gate in the fence.

"Mommy!" she yelled, curls bouncing, skirt flying.

A new flash of memory hit Conn hard.

"Kristy. That's my daughter's name..."

He just stood there as the girl came through the gate and hopped into her mother's arms. Rita buried her face in her daughter's hair, squeezing her until she pulled away, planting a kiss on the child's forehead.

Then the girl sucked in a breath. "I forgot!"

She ran back to the field, where her teacher was holding a majorette's baton.

Meanwhile, it looked as if Rita was daring Conn to say something about her having a daughter. Looked as if she was wondering if this would be enough to let him know that she'd never truly expected him to stay for more than one night in the first place.

How had he reacted when she had told him she had a daughter that night? Had he wanted to run?

But then why would he have taken her necklace and promised to come back? Had he been that much of a jerk that he would've led her on just for another night of great sex?

She watched him wade through all these emotions that he couldn't identify, then finally said, "You remember me telling you about my girl?"

"Yeah. I do now."

"Okay." She looked straight ahead at her daughter. "Then I can't give you any more than that, Conn."

The little girl ran out the gate and Rita took her hand, guiding her away before they could even be introduced.

Conn had checked into the Co-Zee Inn in the more modern east side of town, thinking that he didn't want to crowd Rita too much by checking in to her hotel. He was lying in bed, hoping that his brain would catch up to what he'd experienced today.

As soon as he shut his eyes to the faint neon from the "vacancy" sign bleeding through the green curtains that didn't quite shut all the way, it was as if his mind finally cooperated.

A few memories crept in. *In bed, Rita leaning her head in her hand as she propped herself up with an elbow, her curls spilling down. She was looking down at him as he lay there, using his finger to lazily trace the soft, pale inside of her arm. Their skin was drying from the sweat that had beaded on it during their lovemaking.*

"I usually don't sleep around like this," she said. "I've got responsibilities that I take seriously."

"Like your hotel," he said.

She swallowed hard, her gaze widening, as if what she was about to say next would change everything.

"It's more than that, Conn."

He'd risen up on an elbow, too, coming face-to-face with her.

"Tell me," he said.

"Kristy. That's my daughter's name."

Conn looked into her eyes, expecting that the urge to flee would grab him at any second. Instead, he heard himself saying, "A little girl with your hair and eyes."

Rita seemed as if she thought the night was about to end right there, but...

He leaned toward her, kissed her on the temple, reaching out to slide a hand over her hip...

His eyes opened, his heart beating so fast that he had to sit up to find balance.

Dammit, he'd been smitten by Rita in that moment, hadn't he? But, based on what his brothers had told him, Conn probably would've sent the necklace back to her with an endearment-filled note, finding some charming way to ease their parting while never promising to return after that. He would've used his "Jedi mind tricks," as his oldest brother, Bradon, called it, to make her think that one night of happiness was wonderful enough without expecting more from him.

As he swung his legs over the side of the bed, planting his feet firmly on the shag carpet, he leveled his breathing.

Had he hurt Rita enough to send her into another man's arms? And had *that* man gotten her pregnant and left, too?

Or had the old Conn, the furthest thing from ideal father material, made a baby with her and accidentally left anyway?

As he lay back down, the neon light from the window beat like a red heartbeat on the ceiling.

But it also looked like a warning light, advising him to leave well enough alone.

Chapter Three

The next morning, Rita finished putting Kristy in a leotard for "Job Day" at the preschool. It was Dress Up Week, and right now, at least, Kristy was dressed as a ballerina, her dream career for when she grew up. Last week it'd been a cowgirl like her aunt Kim, the week before, an astronaut.

She wrangled her daughter's curls into a bun using a scrunchy. "Tomorrow you get to wear a princess costume for Royalty Day."

"Pancake Day comes after." Kristy was admiring a beaded pink bracelet around her wrist. "What do I wear for that?"

"Your cutest pajamas, my dear." Rita kissed Kristy's cheek, lingering, loving the sweet smell of her. She still had that little-girl scent, sugar and spice and everything nice, and she hoped it would never go away.

When Conn had walked with her to the preschool yesterday, Rita had at first been reluctant to have him along while she picked up her daughter. But since she'd told him about Kristy "that night," a part of her genuinely wanted to see if he would remember. And if he would get the same look on his face that he'd had after she'd revealed that she was the mother of a four-year-old.

But that was where she'd stopped with the honesty. She'd also had a total knee-jerk, ultradefensive reaction when he'd asked about her little baby bump; she'd outright lied to him that the child wasn't his.

Right afterward, she'd known it wasn't the right thing to do. He was the father. Yet he was also a very scattered man who wouldn't be remotely reliable. He might even be another Kevin, so making Conn think that this was someone else's baby seemed to be the safest choice for both of them.

Even so, Rita kept picturing Conn as he'd been in that bed, while he smiled down at her as if the news about her having a daughter already didn't bother him at all.

"A little girl with your hair and eyes," he'd said before caressing her again, leading her into a place where she could hope and love and forget the past.

Would he be able to show that kind of affection for a surprise baby? Kevin sure hadn't.

Kristy hopped toward her bedroom door. "Can I do the computer now? We brushed my teeth!"

"You sure can." Kristy often got sidetracked by everything *but* getting ready in the morning, so Rita had found that dangling the reward of using the laptop computer was incentive for her to stay focused.

They went to the kitchen table where Rita directed the computer to a kid-friendly page with Barbie games and went to her room to finish her own toilette.

The top floor of the hotel had always been the caretaker's quarters and, even though the property had been handed down, generation after generation, Rita's own family hadn't actually lived in the suite, which was decorated with the same Victorian furniture and antiques that gave the rest of the hotel its Old West feel. It'd been too small for two parents and three children when she was younger.

But it was just right for her and Kristy and another one on the way. The three of them.

She didn't stop to think about how it might've seemed a little more crowded with Kevin, had he stuck around. Or with any other man.

As she got to her bathroom, then pinned back her hair with a barrette, she tried not to think about Conn, but it was impossible not to. What would've happened if he hadn't gotten in that accident? *Would* he have come back?

How long would he have stayed?

Heart muted, she told herself to stop dwelling on it. Instead, she forced her attention to the task of applying a little blush, then eye shadow, mascara, which she seemed low on, and pink lipstick. Then she stifled a yawn as she went to the personal calendar she kept posted on the refrigerator in the kitchen area. It mainly showed Kristy's upcoming activities: Job Day, a slumber party tonight with Aunt Kim, Royalty Day, Pancake Day, dance and baton lessons.

All this in addition to her own schedule, which included a doctor's appointment this week, maid-of-honor duties for Violet's wedding this weekend, then Thanksgiving *next* week. She would definitely have to begin working in more time for her and her unborn baby— nap time so she wouldn't be stressed, a little light exercise time…

Rita thought about the looks she'd been getting around town recently as she strolled the boardwalk, her tummy just beginning to show. Some glanced at her and smiled. Others had an expression on their faces as if thinking, "She never learns, does she?"

Another unplanned pregnancy. And the thing was, Rita was such a careful person. Always had been, too.

With Kevin, she'd been engaged. She hadn't seen him for a while, because he'd needed to relocate near Houston for a job in some natural-gas fields because of the kaolin-mine closure. She'd been so young then, so unsuspecting about how life could go wrong, and she'd thought that she and Kevin would always love each other, that neither of them would ever change.

But he'd grown distant after taking the new job. It'd been a gradual thing, with him being more withdrawn during his weekend visits, with him complaining more and more about the mine closure and how life wasn't fair. Kevin had never done well with change.

Yet Rita had merely told herself that he would get used to life as she worked her rear off in the hopes of taking time away from the hotel and attending college. She had loved him as she had during high school, when they'd been sweethearts, and after graduation, when they'd kept on seeing each other, saving their money for when they would have a family one day.

Then, one night, during a rushed bout of weekend lovemaking, something had happened. Her diaphragm hadn't been inserted as it should've been—at least, that was the doctor's guess. She'd gotten pregnant before getting married and...

Dammit, Rita, we're not ready for a family.

Now, at the memory of Kevin's reaction to the news, Rita turned away from the calendar. Why did it all have to come back?

Kevin demanding that she rethink their situation in life. Kevin "suggesting" that she "take care" of their "mistake." Her finding out that their life had been a lie all along when he told her he had been seeing another woman in his "other home," the one he lived in during the week for his job.

Him leaving Rita as an unmarried mother for that other woman.

Blowing out a breath, Rita told herself that she'd been careful with Conn, too—at least physically. It was just that, when they'd used protection, there'd been one time when the condom had slipped a little after they'd made love and he was pulling out of her...

She rubbed her belly under her work skirt. No matter the circumstances, she was already head over heels for this child. Like Kristy, this baby would be easy to love, to take care of, to hold and kiss and treasure.

I'll always be here, she thought, softly patting her tummy. *But who needs a daddy you can't trust?*

She kept telling herself that Conn didn't even know who he was, so what kind of father could he be? As far as *she* even knew, she'd gone to bed with a fantasy— the Conn Flannigan who had seemed just as taken with her as she'd been with him that night.

That fantasy man didn't exist, though.

Walking down the hall, she heard the sounds from

the computer and went over to Kristy, bending down to plant a long kiss on top of her head. "Come on, sweetie. Time to go."

"One more minute?" the little girl asked.

"Nope. You've still got a half hour banked for computer time this week, though, and you can use it later."

A jaunty knock sounded on the door, and Kristy bounded over to open it. As Rita shut down the computer, Kristy squealed.

"Aunt Kim!"

When Rita glanced over she saw her younger sister, dressed in old boots and jeans and a threadbare blue T-shirt. Kim was wearing her dark curly hair in a ponytail, seeming every inch the tomboy of the family. She lifted Kristy up, twirled her around, then set her back down and used her forefinger to tweak the child's nose.

"Why, if it isn't Tina Ballerina," Kim said.

"*Kristy* Ballerina."

Both Kim and Rita laughed. "Thanks for walking her to school," she said to Kim on the way out the door.

"No problem. It's my day off, anyway, and Nick's got everything covered."

Good ol' big bro.

As Rita shut the door, she braced herself for what the day would bring. Would wagging tongues be spreading news about Conn, with the way he was following her around and holding on to that *R* necklace she'd always worn, ever since she'd bought it from the Whitefeather Jewelry Boutique with her first real paycheck from the hotel?

She hoped he'd finally gone home. At least, part of her did. The other part of her was just plain masochistic, she supposed, because it yearned for him, even after all that had happened.

They all went down the stairs, coming to the lobby, which was empty at this time of the morning.

Except for one person sitting in a velvet-upholstered chair.

Wouldn't you know it, at the sight of Conn, Rita's belly spun into a whir of desire and anxiety. His hat was perched on one bent knee as he perused a brochure about tourist sites in Houston. His hair was so thick and tempting that she bunched her fists, wishing she didn't want to touch him so badly. He'd also taken a razor to his face, which was freshly shaven, emphasizing a strong jaw and cleft chin.

She shivered, thinking of how he'd held her, how he'd been inside of her. How he'd looked down at her as the dawn had rolled through the crack in the curtains. She'd never seen a look like that before, not even from Kevin, and it'd seemed so real.

Real enough to make her believe that he would stay forever.

He glanced up from his reading, as if he had Rita Radar. "Morning," he said ever so casually.

Rita was desperate to make it seem as if he were just another customer. "Morning."

Kristy wasn't fooled, though. By the way she was pressing against her aunt Kim's leg, checking Conn out, she recognized him from yesterday.

Rita kissed her daughter goodbye, then thanked Kim again. There weren't any employees coming in to cover the front desk this morning, so it was up to Rita to do it.

"So we'll see you tomorrow," Kim said, heading for

the exit with Kristy in tow. Then to Kristy, "We're going to have *fun* at our slumber party tonight."

"Yeah!" Kristy said.

Since Kristy visited Kim frequently, there was no need for packing this morning—Kristy had a drawer of clothing, plus a toothbrush, over at her aunt's cabin.

Rita went over and gave Kristy an extra-big kiss. "Call me tonight?"

"Okay, Mommy."

"We'll check in before we have our *Caillou* marathon." Kim gave Conn a curious glance before ushering Kristy to the door.

As for Kristy, she just kept checking out the cowboy.

When they left, the room seemed way too quiet. Rita thought about turning on the radio, until Conn got out of his seat and ambled over to the desk.

"I want to thank you for yesterday," he said. "It helped."

"Good to hear."

Her pulse jittered. The last thing she needed was for all her hot-blooded, ill-thought-out feelings to come bursting up right now.

Good thing his next words put a stop to them. "I keep remembering bits and pieces about that night but... There are things that go along with them that I'm not really understanding, Rita."

Oh, the sound of her name. He had a way of saying it, deep and low. Of owning it, somehow.

But she'd already come to the conclusion during the four months he'd been gone that she'd never be owned— not by another man, not by the anguish she'd managed to tame.

She decided to duck any deeper conversation. It was safer that way. "So your memory's been jarred?"

"Somewhat." His brow furrowed, as if he were on the edge of saying or thinking something that wasn't quite gelling for him. "I could really use more of your help, though. You seem to be some kind of key for me." He added that devastating smile that had gotten her into bed in the first place. "What do you say?"

That smile tugged at her so hard that she had to grip the counter.

He added, "There'd even be a good dinner it in for you after you finish with work."

"Then you'll go home?"

He laughed. "I made arrangements this morning to take some time off from the ranch, so I'm not in any hurry. But I swear I won't bother you anymore after this. I'd just like to wander around town, see if there's anything else here that'll tweak my brain."

"Goody."

He ignored her sarcasm. "Don't tell me you're not free tonight, Rita. I was sitting right here when your sister said she'd be having a slumber party with Kristy."

Shoot. Kim *had* mentioned the aunt/niece outing right in front of him. But there were a million other excuses to get out of this—like her final dress fitting for Vi's wedding early tomorrow, for one. Resting her tired feet, for another.

Yet… She touched her belly. A baby. His baby. Maybe she owed him or her one dinner with the father, just for some closure and a chance to tell him the truth—if she could bring herself to do it.

She gripped the counter even tighter with her free hand. Thing was, she didn't trust herself around this man. Whenever he was within range, her blood heated, her heart twirled, her body urged her to do things she shouldn't even be dreaming of repeating with him.

Ground rules. Maybe she should just make some for him *and* for her.

"If we had dinner tonight," she said, "it wouldn't be anything…"

"Romantic?" He nodded. "I understand."

She couldn't decipher his expression, but the sinking sensation in her chest was real easy to read. Had she actually expected him to beg her to take up where they'd left off? He had to be just as wary of coming back to face her as she was to see him, and just because he was here didn't mean he…

Well, that he remembered that night and the connection she'd thought they had, even just after several hours together.

He backed away from the counter, seemingly satisfied now. While putting his hat back on, he said, "What time's good for you?"

It'd been a long while since she'd gotten ready to go out socially after work, so she calculated quickly. "Six?"

"Six it is."

"There's a good fish shack by Dempsy Lake, south of town. The Levee, they call it." It was very public, although a little bit off the beaten track in St. Valentine itself, and usually populated by families during the afternoons she'd been there.

"Sounds good." He sent her that grin again.

As he tipped his hat to her and went out the doorway, she held her breath.

And, for the rest of the day, it felt as if she never let it go.

* * *

The sky was rumbling softly when Conn drove Rita in his rented Ford truck down a winding dirt road to The Levee.

It was a semi-awkward drive, too, with the radio on, humming old Trisha Yearwood songs in place of conversation. He figured they'd have enough of that at the restaurant, so he didn't push Rita into talking.

In fact, he didn't think it wise to push her into anything—not this skittish woman. And if he had to take half of their meal to get her comfortable, he would sure do that, too.

But truthfully, he also didn't mind the notion of merely spending time with her. His libido certainly didn't object. Hell, it'd just about gone crazy when Rita had met him in front of the hotel, where she'd been waiting in a long flowing dark skirt and silver sweater with a thick wrap, perfect for a moonlit, rainy fall night. Her hair was pulled back in a barrette, wildly curling.

When they arrived at the fish shack, he scanned the stretched cabin that perched over the lake, which glittered under the fall of tiny raindrops. Pines surrounded the water, lending a heady fragrance.

He stood back as Rita took the stairs up to the wrap-around porch, with its wooden rockers and a cigar-store totem pole out front, then he followed. Inside, the furnishings were simple, but it was the view that dominated the room.

Long windows, the shimmering lake.

Candlelit romance.

Rita seemed to realize that she might've picked the wrong location as they obeyed the sign by the hostess desk saying, "Take a seat."

"It sure doesn't look like this during the afternoon," she said quietly, heading for a lakeside table away from most of the other diners in the room, who'd gravitated toward the side where the view of the water was the best.

He pulled out a simple knotted-pine chair with a gingham cushion and waited for her to sit. Then he went to his own place across the small table and grabbed menus from the silver holders, giving one to her first.

"You come here often?" he asked.

"Not since…" She shrugged. "It's been a while."

Had she come here on dates? With friends back when she hadn't shouldered the burden of running the hotel?

The waiter, with his blue-and-white checked shirt and a gap-toothed smile, was quick in taking their orders.

Rita fidgeted with her paper napkin before spreading it over her lap. Yeah, it definitely wasn't time to grill her. She looked ready to jump out of her chair at his slightest misstep.

"St. Valentine looks like a nice place to have grown up," he said. A totally neutral, totally safe topic.

She seemed surprised that he hadn't rushed right into the meat of the matter. "It was very nice…when I was a kid. It was almost like the most beautiful chapters of a book like *To Kill a Mockingbird*—the parts without Boo Radley and Atticus Finch's court case. Summers in swimming holes, adventures in old, abandoned houses. Things like that."

"It *was* nice?" Was he treading on thin ice even by asking? Was he getting too personal for what his business was with her?

She didn't seem to mind. "I say it *was* nice because

the older I got, the more I realized just how small the town is. The favorite pastime tends to be getting into other people's business. But I guess that comes with having everyone see you grow up and take part in your life."

He was about to ask what she could've done to whip up any gossip in the past, before this mysterious pregnancy, but then he thought of Kristy, and of how that father seemed to be out of the picture, too.

Rita was playing with her napkin again, so he got the signal and shifted the topic.

"You said that your family has always owned that hotel."

"Right." There—she let go of the napkin, smiled up at the waiter as he brought them the drinks they had ordered. "My great-grandpa came over from Portugal with my grandmother in the early 1930s. That was just after Tony Amati officially made it St. Valentine."

Hell, this wasn't awkward at *all*. "So you're a St. Valentine institution."

"Most everyone in Old Town is. But the kaolin-mine closure several years ago shook things up. It's taken years to get back on our feet, and we lost some of our population when the unemployed miners went off to a natural-gas operation near Houston."

"That's why Old Town seems like a ghost town?"

"Right. There's also a social line running between Old Town mining families and the new richies." She raised an eyebrow. "I guess the Niles clan falls somewhere in the middle."

He couldn't believe he'd actually gotten her to talking. "When you run a small business like your family, I guess it doesn't pay to take sides."

She glanced out the window as rain tapped against it. The soft candlelight burnished her skin, and he longed to run his fingertips over the smoothness. The slope of her cheekbones fascinated him. So did her lips.

He kept watching them as she spoke, a pit of yearning in his belly.

"I'd ask you all about where you grew up," she said, "except you already told me."

And there she was, talking about what he needed her to talk about. She had come around after all.

"Listen, I know that you probably didn't tell me everything yesterday when we talked because you wanted me to scram, but was there anything else I shared with you that night? Even the smallest detail might trigger another memory."

She adjusted the silverware in front of her. "I can offer just a few more tidbits. Like when you said something about majoring in procrastination during college while you got an ag business degree. You also said that your grandpa built up your cattle ranch, and after your dad passed on years ago, you and your three brothers took it over, along with your mom. You all have your own parcel of land, a cabin, a place of your own. You sounded…very content."

The observation sounded distant, though, as if he'd never be able to get to that point again.

"Conn," she said. "We didn't spend enough time together for me to know all your ins and outs. Even though…"

"Even though what?"

She pressed her lips together just as the waiter came with their fish-and-chips platters. After he left, she shook a little bit of salt and vinegar onto her meal.

"Rita," he asked, "did I do something besides take your necklace and tell you I'd be back?"

"Like propose marriage after one night?" She laughed. "No. But I guess I thought there was a...connection."

The words had tumbled out of her, as if she'd been holding on to them too long and just wanted to get rid of them now. She kept her head down, obviously not wanting to see his expression.

"I don't know what to say." He wanted to use a finger to tilt up her chin so he could look into her beautiful, clear gray eyes—as clear as he remembered from that night.

"Don't feel guilty, Conn. I made it through that day or two of disappointment just fine."

"I can see that."

She looked up. Were her eyes a little glassy?

Dammit, he didn't want her to cry, and anger crawled up inside him. He hated himself for doing this to her. Hated that he didn't know exactly how he'd felt that night, because his wisps of memory only got him so far.

Hated that he might've just been stringing her along, as he'd reportedly done with other women.

So why was there something buzzing around in his chest? What the hell was it that had made her face such an important part of trying to remember—a face powerful enough to have brought him back to St. Valentine?

She ignored her food. "Just so you know, I'm not being remote on purpose. I want to help. It's only..."

He waited her out, his heart beating.

She sighed. "It's just how I am."

And there it was—a major warning. A signal that,

even if the candlelight and murmuring rain got to them, nothing would ever happen with Rita again.

Disappointment nipped at him, even though rekindling their brief encounter was the last thing either of them needed.

She continued in the same level voice. "Kristy's father left me about five years ago. We'd dated throughout high school and then afterward, until we got engaged. Neither of us were well-off. We lived hand-to-mouth, really, and that's why we took so long to get married. We wanted to save our money—him with his mining job, me with working at the hotel. Then, as you know, the mine closed."

"But he got a job in the natural-gas field, right?"

"Right. But something significant had already changed for him by then."

Conn got a bad feeling about where this was going.

"We didn't plan to get pregnant. *I* was happy about it. We'd only have to work a little harder to make ends meet. He flipped out, though."

"Did he…?"

She nodded. "He wanted an abortion. I didn't. And I couldn't believe that the man I thought I loved was asking for one. I had no idea who he was anymore. But he kept up the emotional pressure."

"And he left when he didn't get his way."

"He had a bit on the side. Another woman who wasn't half the trouble Kristy and I would've been." Her gaze was full of shadows. "But that ended up for the best."

Conn narrowed his eyes. Would the old Conn have taken off, too, in the same situation?

Her face brightened. "I'm raising Kristy by myself. It isn't easy sometimes, with running the hotel, too, but it's worth it. And my brother and sister help out as much as they can."

Their conversation went full circle for him now. "And that's why St. Valentine stopped being that beautiful summertime place for you—because of how life turned out."

When she looked into his eyes, he could see that she was more guarded than ever.

"Everyone in town knows how my life turned out, too, down to the last detail, it seems," she said. "And you know how some people in small towns can be—nosey, judgmental, always thinking they know best for an unmarried woman who should've known better than to make trouble for herself."

"What exactly happened with the father of this baby?" he asked. Anticipation was a cold wire thrumming through him.

Rita hesitated so long that he started to believe she would never answer.

But even before she did, his nerves were screaming.

"This father," she said, "is just as undependable as my ex-fiancé was, and the last thing I want is to hurt this baby by having him be a part of his or her life."

Chapter Four

The second the words came out of her mouth, she wanted to take them back.

But they were the bald truth.

Rita glanced down at her uneaten plate of food. She'd rather be sharply forthright than to keep lying about the baby's paternity. Sugarcoating the situation wouldn't make things better for them. Good God, Conn didn't even know who he was or where he'd been. He couldn't possibly be together enough to make a decent father.

There was more than even that to consider, too. Besides being a stranger to himself, he was one to her. How could they possibly raise a child under those circumstances?

Maybe, based on what he already knew about himself, he would let her off the hook and go home, continuing his search for who he was. He would have a chance to get back in control of his life again without any other pressures, like a surprise child. And she would be free to raise this baby just as well as she was raising Kristy.

Conn hadn't moved a muscle the entire time, but now he blinked. "Just who is the father, Rita?"

She tucked an errant curl behind her ear, composing herself before looking back up at him. "You are."

"I see." He glanced out the window, swallowing, then turned back to her. "I thought you said—"

"I changed my mind about telling you."

Obviously, his mind was barely keeping up with everything that was hitting it, and a few moments trudged past.

Then he said, "I'm not very good at telling how far along a woman is." He wrinkled his brow. "I'm used to life on a ranch, but not…"

"With a wife or steady girlfriend?"

Her comment must have cuffed him, because he reared back slightly. She'd hit a mark, but it hadn't been because she wanted to be cruel.

It was just that she was made to be a mother, even if there wasn't a father around. Who cared what kind of family she had or how she'd gotten it, just as long as she had one?

But Conn? She was pretty sure he was the opposite, and she would be doing him a favor by cutting him loose.

"I don't hold you to anything," she said. "We had no commitments."

"You think I'm *that* unreliable?"

Slowly, she nodded. "Yes, I do."

It was as if the air had gotten heavier, the raindrops on the window louder, taking over the growing space between them. She drank her water, he drank his, but neither of them ate a bite.

Finally, though, Conn lowered his voice so that she almost didn't hear it. "You don't know if it's a boy or a girl yet?"

She swallowed away the ache in her throat. "No. They tell me I can find out during my next appointment." During all life's craziness, she'd almost forgotten that she was going to the doctor the day after tomorrow. "I've told Dr. Ambrose that I want to be surprised at the birth. It's like…"

"Opening a gift on your own birthday."

When she glanced up, she found him grinning, a look in his eyes that nearly slammed her to the ground.

A…softness?

What was it exactly?

A tiny, wishful thrill spun through her until she throttled it. This was no time for those fantasies she'd entertained about him the first night they'd met. He *wasn't* her dream man, and she sure as heck wasn't some princess who'd been swept away to some happily-ever-after with him.

At any rate, he was taking the news pretty well. Maybe this pregnancy had triggered another memory in him and he was thinking that it *would* be a good idea to leave the baby to her?

She ignored the leaden feeling weighing on her chest. "I guess a birthday present would be a good comparison. But, even though I want to wait, I can't help wishing I could decide on baby names and start buying those teeny-tiny outfits for him or her. Sometimes the temptation to know just gets to me."

"Baby names." There was that tender light in Conn's

gaze again, and it made her wonder if he had ever thought about having children.

If he even remembered thinking about it.

And that was when she lost it—the control she'd been holding on to with such fierceness. It broke, just like that, when she made an attempt to change the subject, segueing into something safe like his life on his cattle ranch or something.

Too bad her attempt to start that new topic sounded just as cracked as her heart.

Cutting herself off, she looked down at her plate again. Dammit, he couldn't see her like this. Not this stranger.

"Rita…"

Her hand had been resting on the table, and she felt Conn's long fingers ease over hers.

At the spinning flip in her belly, she startled in her seat, a catch in her breathing. The warmth of his skin seeped into hers, and she fought the urge to pull back, to let him know without any doubt that touching her really wasn't a good idea.

But she found herself just sitting there, nearly shivering as she hungered for more. As she remembered that night and how his hands had explored places far more sensual.

Don't you dare look up at him right now, she told herself. *Don't do it.…*

Yet she was doing it, her gaze meeting the deep blue of his own—a tender, heartfelt shade that matched the one she'd seen the night they'd been together.

Suddenly, it was as if no time or hard feelings had passed between them at all. He really was a dream who'd walked into the Queen of Hearts Saloon, coming to a cocky stand at her table, grinning and stealing her should-know-better heart.

He must have felt it, too, because he reached across their small, far-too-intimate candlelit table, grasping her hand between the two of his as he leaned forward in his seat.

"I hate to see you sad," he whispered.

Every sound in the restaurant diminished under the low silver light from the moon-glow windows, under the gentleness of his words and gaze.

She wanted to tell him that she wasn't sad—that she had a beautiful child who made every day brighter, plus another one on the way. But there was an inexplicable emptiness inside her, letting her know that something *else* was missing, and it was this emptiness that he probably sensed right now as he stroked a thumb over the sensitive spot near her wrist.

Closing her eyes, Rita tried to find some trace of oxygen in the room so it could fill her lungs and get her breathing again. But there didn't seem to be any.

How could he do this to her when she'd tried so hard to keep it from happening?

Unexpectedly, a tear escaped from her eye before she even knew it was there. It rolled down her cheek, marking her.

"Dammit, Rita."

That tear must have been his undoing, because the next thing she knew, he brought her hand to his lips, resting her wrist there, her pulse tapping against the softness and heat of his mouth.

"I wish everything could work out for the both of us," he murmured against her skin.

And when he reached across the table to rest his

fingers on her face, to touch the trail of her tear, she bit her lip.

It was trembling, just as if she was a girl who'd never had a first time with any man, much less a dangerous one like this.

Now the look in his eyes had turned to something else, heating up like the most searing part of a flame. The part you never played with.

But here she was, wanting to do it.

As she closed her eyes again, leaning into his hand, allowing her lips to barely make contact with his palm, she realized that wanting was the most important thing in the world. Forget control. Forget safety. This was what mattered, because if you didn't feel, you didn't live.

God, how she wanted to live.

In the next slow, endless moment, she felt him lean even closer—close enough so that she could feel his breath over her mouth.

Then...

On a stifled moan, his mouth brushed over hers, sweetly, with just a hint of the blue heat she'd seen in his eyes. Lust—or whatever it'd been that had gotten her into his bed in the first place—roared inside her.

She was so ready—had been ready since he'd left her waiting for him to return.

But then, as if he'd been burned himself, he pulled away.

She couldn't help opening her eyes, seeing him again, finding that his gaze had changed once more, this time to something unfocused, as if...

As if he were remembering.

As if whatever it was that had flashed across his brain had confused the hell out of him.

"What is it?" she asked, feeling the furious blush on her skin and wishing it wasn't there.

Conn paused. He was the one who was looking away from her now, as if he didn't want her to read him.

"It's…" He pressed his lips together, shook his head. "It's nothing."

"Oh." *Had* a memory been triggered? One he didn't want to share?

Rita leaned back in her chair, distancing herself, cursing her weakness in succumbing to him, even if it was just for a moment. What had she been doing?

Duh. The answer was easy, wasn't it? She'd completely forgotten herself and put herself in the exact same place she'd been in that night, when he'd charmed the pants off her and then broken her heart.

Was she crazy, setting herself up again for a repeat performance? And this time the stakes were much higher.

Rita straightened in her chair. Next time she would do everything within her power to make sure nothing like this happened again.

No. Correction. There wouldn't *be* a next time.

She folded her napkin and set it on the table. "If it's all the same, I'd like to box up the food."

When he opened his mouth to argue, she held up a hand.

"This was a mistake. I think we both know it, too."

"I didn't mean to…" He gritted his jaw, then loosened it. "I meant it when I said that I didn't like to see you sad. I got carried away. That's all it was, Rita."

"Okay."

And that was all she really had to say, because it seemed as if she didn't believe him...and as if he maybe didn't even believe it himself.

She sighed. "You and I both know that neither of us can afford to get carried away."

He stared out the window again, just as the rain picked up, throwing itself against the glass. Then, with a nod, he agreed with her, his lips forming a grim line, his jaw tight. A little piece of her heart seemed to break away from the rest of her once again, and she promised herself that this would be the last time her heart would crumble.

Definitely the last time.

She drew in a breath, but it only made her feel the ache in her chest that much more keenly.

"I hope you have everything you need," she said.

For some reason, it seemed as if she'd struck him.

"I told you before—if I have any responsibilities where you're concerned, I'm going to be a man who'll take care of them."

She cradled her tummy, as if securing her heart. "You don't have any responsibilities, Conn. I *want* this baby, and the best thing you can do is to let me raise him or her in a stable home. I provided one for Kristy, and I'll do it again."

His brow furrowed. "So that's it then?"

"Don't you think that's it?"

A storm brewed in his gaze, and she could tell that her words had knifed into him. All he knew was that he was a playboy, a lighthearted bachelor who might provide a bad example as a father.

Shoulders tight, he signaled for the waiter as Rita waited for him to say something else.

But he never did, and an uneasy feeling washed through her, just as surely as the rain was streaking down the windows like tears that she refused to cry anymore.

The road back to Conn's home the next morning seemed longer than it actually was.

The rain had eased off, drying the asphalt that speared through the pastures and white fencing on his way to the Shadow Creek Ranch, where he would be able to retreat to his cabin and finally move on with life.

His brother Emmet had come back to St. Valentine to pick him up a couple of hours ago, and they'd remained quiet so far, listening to the crisp wind whistle through a seal near a window that needed some mending. But that didn't stop Emmet from sneaking looks over at Conn every so often, curious as hell about what had gone on while he was away.

Finally, about a half hour from the ranch, Emmet could stand it no longer.

"You're driving me loco, Conn. Don't you have anything to say?"

"Nope. I got as much as I could out of a visit to St. Valentine, and it's nothing to chat about."

Bullshit. All that'd gone on was that he'd learned he was going to be a father. And that the mother thought he wasn't fit for it.

Worst of all, in spite of her blunt words, he'd gone and stolen a kiss from her.

But how could Conn tell anyone about all that when he didn't understand half of it himself?

He'd been pained by what she'd said about him, but he couldn't refute any of it—not when all he heard from his brothers was about his playboy past and how he was an expert at enjoying himself with women but not tying himself to them.

But…a baby.

Something like fear seized him, making him think that Rita had been right to point out his unsuitability. Maybe it wouldn't be fair to a child to put all his issues on him or her. Maybe he would even end up complicating Rita's life when she already had everything under control, the picture of a loving mom who didn't seem to need a partner to raise a well-adjusted daughter.

Hell, just look at how he'd even reacted with her, giving her that impulsive kiss. It'd been ill-advised, but at the same time, it'd rocked Conn from head to toe, and not just in a physical way.

There'd been a flicker of memory that had never turned into a full-fledged image. But, more important, something had come loose in Conn, causing a mini-avalanche of feelings he was still trying to grasp.

An overwhelming flood of affection and…well, questions. Hopes. Things like a deep yearning to… Do what?

The answer was balancing on an edge inside of Conn, and it frustrated the hell out of him that he couldn't shake that one memory loose.

Didn't this just go to prove the instability that Rita had pointed out?

That was the reason he'd left.

Emmet gave him another long look, and Conn rolled his eyes.

"Jeez…*what?*"

"Something's just off about you." Emmet returned his gaze to the road. "You've always been a lone wolf when it comes to keeping most of your thoughts to your-self, but this is ridiculous."

He was getting annoyed with his brothers always reminding him of who he'd been. "Why do you keep pointing out my worst qualities? Has it ever occurred to you that I might've left them behind?"

"Because you've forgotten them?"

Conn didn't say anything for a moment. Then he narrowed his eyes, looking out the window at the pass-ing oaks curled over the country road, constructing a sparse tunnel of sorts. "The old Conn could come back, but I'm not sure I can warm up to him. If he gave all those women he seduced a bad attitude like he did Rita, then I have to assume he didn't care much about them in the first place. He didn't seem to treat women very well, for one thing."

And just imagine how he might treat a baby. Like a toy that he would leave behind when it lost its shininess?

Emmet grinned wryly. "Oh, but you did treat them well, Conn. At the time. I told you before, though—you had a graceful way of getting out of any serious entan-glements and you left the girls happy."

"How do you know that for certain? Did you ever meet any of those women?"

Emmet shrugged. "Can't say I ever did. But you al-ways made it sound as if you left them smiling."

Another stretch of road ran by the window as they abandoned the oaks and the gray sky appeared, reflect-ing the color of Rita's eyes.

He could only hope he'd left the *other* women smil-ing.

Emmet laid off Conn the rest of the way, and it wasn't too long before they pulled into the road that ran past the main Colonial-style house on the Shadow Creek Ranch—four hundred and fifty acres of land that housed Brahman cattle.

Emmet pulled into the driveway, next to two beat-up trucks that belonged to their older brothers. "Mom's got lunch going. She wanted to see you before you holed up in your cabin for a rest."

"I don't need a nap."

"Don't argue that with Mom. She's got doctors' recommendations on her side."

Conn just about bit his tongue as he got out of the truck. There were a million things to do now that he was back. But who was he to go against the Word of Mom?

They went around the back, where an herb garden preceded a deck where Bradon and Dillon, Conn's oldest brothers, were sitting in lawn chairs under the cloudy sky. Their boys—all three of them—came bounding over from their spot off the side of the deck, where they'd been digging in the dirt with plastic toys.

"Uncle Conn!"

Bradon's five-year-old twins bashed into Conn's legs first, followed by Dillon's waddling toddler. They all hugged Conn, nearly toppling him.

"Whoa," he said, laughing, patting them on their shoulders. "I wasn't gone that long."

"Yes, you were!" shouted Nate, the more outgoing twin.

"Yeah!" Ned, his brother, echoed him. "We missed you!"

Meanwhile, Conn ruffled their two-year-old cousin Jacob's thick dark hair—a feature that didn't escape any of the Flannigan brood.

Ned tugged on Conn's shirtsleeve. "Want to dig worms with us?"

Dillon spoke up. "I'm sure Conn would rather sit and have a beer. Right?"

Conn shrugged. "Maybe later, kid." He winked at the twins, and they scrambled off to do some more worm harassing. Jacob did his best to catch up with them, the sight of such short legs in baggy jeans making Conn chuckle.

But his laughter died when he thought of another child—the baby. Rita's baby.

His baby.

He brushed off the thought, because, as Rita said, it was for the best that he was here and she was there.

Wasn't it?

"Hey," Bradon said, standing up and coming over to Conn so he could hand him a beer. "You plan to just stand there all day?"

With one smooth move, Emmet walked out from behind Conn and scooped the beer out of Bradon's hand. "Don't mind if I do."

Bradon chuckled, then lightly pushed Conn toward the table with brotherly affection. Burlier than any of the brothers, he'd been the football star in the family—a fullback—until his knee had given out during an All-American game and destroyed his dreams of going pro.

Dillon was the baseball master—a pretty good pitcher—but his heart had always been on the ranch, much like Emmet's and Conn's. He'd even married his childhood sweetheart, Hayley, before settling on Shadow Creek for good in their own cabin, just as each brother owned.

"Any luck in St. Valentine?" he asked.

"Got a few mental nudges," Conn said as Bradon cracked open another beer and handed it over. He briefly told them about Rita, leaving out most of the details. Hell—a lot of the details. "Day by day, flashes are coming to me, but…"

"But it's not enough," Dillon said, compassion written all over his tanned face. He tipped back his cowboy hat and took a sip of beer.

Conn took a swig too, then said, "I don't think flashes will ever be enough. Not until they make one big picture of the past."

Emmet sat back in his chair and propped a booted foot over his knee. "Funny. There're a lot of people who'd love a clean slate in life."

"Like you?" Bradon asked.

"My life's perfect." Emmet saluted them with his bottle. "Nothing else I ever wanted but to be free under an open Texas sky, and I've got that in spades."

As he drank, Conn wondered if Emmet was being facetious. It was his brother's tone that made him second-guess.

The creak of an opening screen door turned their attention toward the house, where Mom stood in the doorway.

"I see our wanderer is back," she said, her hand on a curvy hip that was covered by an apron that read Goddess of the Hearth. Her dark hair glinted with silver streaks, cut in a short, no-fuss style.

"Mom," Conn said, rising to go to her, then hugging her.

She was stronger than she looked as she embraced him right back. "How did it go?"

He used his stock answer. "Fine. During lunch I'll tell you the little I accomplished."

"Good. The girls are inside, seeing to the last touches." She was talking about Trixie and Hayley, Bradon's and Dillon's wives. "It's time for y'all to come in and wash up, though." She motioned toward the boys. "I don't want any dirty angels at my table."

As she went back through the door, he caught a whiff of home—meat loaf, vegetables and fresh-baked bread. The wafting aroma must've gotten to his brothers, too, because they were already out of their seats, urging Conn inside.

He managed to get through the meal with just as many scant details as he'd offered Emmet on the ride home and, after they'd gotten their fill, Conn had Emmet drop him off at his place. As his brother pulled away, Conn merely nodded a goodbye to his brother, mostly to thank Emmet for staying mum about his adventures with Rita—sleeping with her, and even getting her pregnant, if Emmet suspected anything about it. Once inside the log cabin, which he'd built with his brothers over the years until he'd moved into it in his early twenties, he tossed his duffel bag on his quilted mattress in the bedroom and unzipped it.

He pulled out jeans, socks, a couple of shirts, aiming to toss them in his hamper, just as something fell out of the bundle and clanked to the wooden floor.

Conn didn't move as he caught a glimpse of Rita's necklace, with the *R* split in two.

Like gold lightning, an image hit him, whisking him away. *His lips brushing hers, a pow of agonized need tearing through him, a craving so strong that all he wanted to do was hold on to it...*

It was the kiss from last night. But that wasn't all. On its tail came another flash, and suddenly, he was engrossed in an older memory.

White-wedding frills and church flowers. Sitting with his mom in a pew as Bradon stood at the altar with his bride, Trixie. Mom dabbing at her eyes with a linen handkerchief, leaning over to whisper, "It's out there for you, too, Conn. I found it with my Owen, bless his soul, and all you have to do is look a little harder."

Then, another memory—one that clashed with the first.

The morning after, with Rita in bed still sleeping, the early light whispering through a gap in the curtain as he thought, I've got to have more from her....

The mental pictures slipped away to nothing just as quickly as they'd come and, after a second, Conn bent down to get the necklace.

It gleamed in his palm. What had the memories meant? Could they mean that, when he'd left Rita that morning, he truly *had* intended to come back?

But for just how long?

Rattled, Conn sat on the bed. Strange, how these memories had come one right after the other: His mom telling him that he was going to find love, then him, looking down at a sleeping Rita in bed. The connection didn't make sense, especially if he only meant to have a brief affair with her.

Frustration chewed on him once again. This was just like last night, when the post-kiss memory had only begun to inch toward a precipice, toward a fall where everything might finally crash down and jar him into true reality.

But he still wasn't there. Even now, he was being teased by bits and pieces.

Conn looked down at the necklace in his hand, seeing how the *R* still hadn't come together, knowing that with just one push, it could very well become whole again.

A real man—a man who had himself together— would push.

So who was Connall Flannigan? More important, who did he *want* to be?

Didn't he have a choice in the matter?

He pushed the necklace together so it formed a solid letter.

R for Rita.

And that's when he knew.

"Let's get a good look at your bundle of joy," said Dr. Ambrose as she waited for Rita to push her sweats just low enough for her curved belly to protrude over the waistband.

She lay back on the table in the exam room, tugging up her loose pink sweatshirt. "I thought things would be more difficult with this pregnancy," she said while the doctor rubbed gel over her tummy. "The only minor complaint I have is that I tend to get dizzy sometimes when I get up too quickly. That's about it, though."

Dr. Ambrose, who'd been Rita's practitioner since she was a child, nodded. "You should make it a point to relax more."

"I will. I've got a lot of things coming up, like Vi's wedding this weekend, and the rehearsal dinner and bachelorette party tonight. But I definitely won't overdo it."

"Good. Are you eating enough protein? Sometimes your blood sugar is affected when you don't get enough of it, or if you're not eating regularly."

"I'll make sure I'm doing that, too. Otherwise, I'm feeling really good this time around. Kristy exhausted me. I slept all the time and was always moody."

The doctor gave her an understanding smile. She didn't have to say that Rita had been going through some massive troubles during Kristy's pregnancy, just after Kevin had revealed his affair and he'd left them both in the cold.

Rita tried not to think that, maybe, the doctor was even wearing a little of that caring, yet definitely chafing, "You should've known better" expression that everyone else in St. Valentine seemed to have, too.

She exhaled. Paranoid. That's what she was. Dr. Ambrose had always been considerate and never said an annoying word to her. It was just that, ever since Conn had come around—and especially after he'd left again—she'd sensed that people on the streets were monitoring her, just as they'd done when she'd gotten pregnant the first time.

Conn. She could still feel his kiss, the gentleness of it, and there was that masochistic part of her that wanted him here to see his baby on the screen.

But fat chance of that. She'd chased him off well and good.

"You'll do just fine, Rita," the doctor said in her soothing, maternal voice. She even wore her faded brown hair in a relaxed granny bun that had a pencil sticking out of it, and her kind blue eyes were rayed by laugh lines. "All pregnancies are different. Don't create problems by worrying about why nothing is wrong with this pregnancy."

As Dr. Ambrose put the transducer against Rita's tummy, she tried to relax, but failed.

She was still wanting Conn here. Still somewhat regretting that he wasn't, even though it was for the best.

"Perfect as they come," the doctor said.

Rita peered at the monitor to find a sweet little huddled shape. Tears gathered in her throat. "The baby's perfect?" Just as perfect as that one night with Conn had been, when she'd thought that he might be the type of man who would love her?

"Perfect," the doctor said.

The sound of her child's heartbeat filled the room, and it pulsed through Rita, too.

It was silly, maybe even strange, but she pictured Conn standing by her side, watching the monitor right along with her. What would his face look like as he listened to the cadence of his child's heartbeat, as he saw this miracle that had happened between them?

She pictured him, the proudest dad on earth, unable to look away from the screen, but...

But then she realized that, besides Dr. Ambrose and the baby, she was the only person in the room.

All alone.

Was it worth it? Was she doing the right thing, assuming that Conn was too much of a disaster right now to handle a baby?

She got a grip on herself as she watched the tiny person on the screen—legs, arms, toes, fingers. All so small. All so vulnerable.

Yes, this was the right thing to do. What if, after

Conn regained his memories, he *did* become another Kevin?

That's not what this baby needed, much less Kristy....

Rita listened to the heartbeat a little more, hoping it would make her feel better. It did, and it didn't.

Fortunately, Dr. Ambrose spoke. "If you want to know your baby's sex, I can tell you."

Rita remembered what Conn had said when they'd had dinner last night. "It's like opening a gift on your own birthday."

God help her, she wanted to see what was inside.

"Yes," she said, her voice thick. "I really want to know."

Dr. Ambrose smiled that motherly smile. "You've got another little girl on the way, Rita."

She laughed in utter joy. A girl. And, before she could stop herself, she looked at the place beside her, where she'd imagined Conn standing earlier.

A little girl. Our little girl...

But, of course, he wasn't there.

Chapter Five

"Why a wedding just before Thanksgiving?" Rita murmured as she rushed out of the general store the next day, garbed in the first pair of sweats she'd seen in her dresser and with her hair pushed up into a messy bun. It'd been a chaotic morning, with her not only having to pick up some mascara, since she'd run out of it, but with her sister Kim arriving a little late to watch over Kristy, who was in one of her feistier moods. This, after yesterday, with the doctor's appointment, a weekly inspection of the hotel, the rehearsal dinner and a short stint at Vi's bachelorette party *plus* menu planning for the Thanksgiving that she and Kristy would be spending alone, since Kim and Nick would be en route to a horse-breeding schmooze-fest with some very good customers from out of the country.

While aiming for the church, Rita made sure that

her garment bag, filled with her maid-of-honor dress, didn't drag on the ground. She was also trying to carry a satchel with her shoes and accessories.

But those weren't even the biggest things she was pulling around.

Nope—she wasn't going to think about Conn right now. Wasn't. Going. To.

She didn't have time for the pang of missing him, for imagining that, for once, he might've gotten to see her all dolled up and looking like more than a hotel desk clerk if she hadn't chased him out of town.

She didn't have time for wanting.

Drawing near the church, she saw that someone had already adorned the white picket fence with autumn-hued decorations. Vi had wanted a fall wedding, and she'd chosen Thanksgiving time since some out-of-town relatives would already be visiting the area. Mist hung in the air, as if waiting for the sun to burn it off, while Rita entered the gate to the courtyard. She rounded the church to go to a side door where, in a half hour, she was to meet her hairdresser, who was going to make sense of this rat's nest on top of her head.

But when she saw who was sitting on the stoop, she came to an abrupt halt.

Conn Flannigan spied her at the same time, slowly rising to his feet while taking off his cowboy hat.

All six-foot-plus of him. All tall, dark and off-limits, if she had any brains whatsoever.

"Rita," he said, and the sound of his voice flowed through her, gathering in the center of her chest where it thudded.

He was looking at her as if she wasn't the total mess

she knew she was, dressed in the drabbest clothing possible and…

Good God, she wasn't even wearing any makeup yet. Altogether, she felt more vulnerable than ever in front of him.

"What are you doing here?" she blurted out. Heck, it almost sounded like an accusation, as if he had some nerve seeing her like this.

He laughed a little. "Hi to you, too."

She fought the urge to run, because she was basically au natural and, hello, he was seeing what she *really* looked like when she rolled out of bed. On the morning after their one-night stand, at least she'd still had on a trace of makeup.

He remained on the stoop, as if he was facing a skittish creature and he didn't want to make her bolt. "I heard about Vi's wedding this morning when I grabbed breakfast at the Orbit Diner. I figured you might be a part of it…"

"And you came to the church." Yay.

"I actually went to your hotel first, but the clerk said you were already gone. So I took a chance and waited here."

Took a chance, Rita thought. She'd already taken one too many of those with him.

But with him only about eight feet away, close enough for her to be under his spell once again, she felt as if she would take a thousand chances if only her common sense would let her.

Luckily, she still had *that*.

"You haven't told me why you're still here," she said. "I didn't think you'd stick around."

"I left, but I couldn't stay away."

A slam of emotion hit her, almost as if she'd been putting pedal to the metal, driving so fast that she hadn't seen what was ahead of her and crashed—but in a good way. It took her a moment to actually feel the happiness that his words brought on.

He couldn't stay away?

But just as soon as she thought it, he corrected himself.

"What I meant to say is that I came to a realization at home. A decent man wouldn't stay away in this situation."

Somehow, she kept herself standing upright. Was he talking about the baby? Or was there something else he was referring to?

It was too much to hope that he'd come back because he had all of a sudden remembered everything his amnesia had taken away from him, and he'd realized that their one night had been chock-full of true love.

"What exactly do you mean?" she asked.

"The baby you're carrying is mine, Rita. That should tell you everything."

Although there was a warm spot growing in the pit of her stomach at that news, she withered a little, too.

Of course he hadn't come back just for her. Who ever did?

Yet shouldn't the fact that he'd returned because of their baby make her happy in and of itself? He was here because he didn't want to leave her in the lurch. He was every bit the good man she'd hoped he was.

Wasn't he?

"So," she said, her voice sounding so tiny, "you're here because of some notion of honor then."

He seemed to turn that over in his mind, then a long

breath escaped him before he said, "Maybe it is honor. I have a feeling I never had much of it."

He glanced at her as if she knew enough about him to tell him otherwise, but she only shook her head. That haunted look she'd seen on him so many times took up residence in his gaze again, and she almost closed the distance between them, comforting him.

But the space that separated them was too big in so many ways.

"I kept thinking of you and this child," he said, "and it was out of the question for me to stay home."

He met her gaze straight on, but she didn't back down. Her past wouldn't allow her to.

"Do you even want to be a dad?" she asked.

"I think I could be a good one."

It was an analytical answer, but what else could she expect from a man whose life was in flux? She would bet he wasn't even sure what kind of emotions he should be having—what emotions the "real him" would have.

"I don't understand," she said, finally stepping forward and dropping her bag to the stoop—except for her dress. She kept that in front of her like a thin shield. "I'm not holding you to anything. You could go on with your life and not be saddled."

"Then I guess we have some things to talk over, because that's not my plan."

He was impossible. "How can you even want this in your condition?"

"How?" He looked genuinely puzzled. "How can I not?"

As he said it, she could see something in his eyes grow stronger, and she wasn't sure just why that was.

He still had to be confused, right? Like Kevin, he

would end up not wanting the responsibility, and she had to prepare for the inevitability of that.

"You don't know what you're asking for," she said. "You're going through a lot, Conn. Maybe you're—"

"Not thinking straight?" Now he sounded angry.

"I think you're dealing with more than any human should have to deal with. You've still got a lot to sort out."

And that's what makes you extra dangerous to me.

He gripped his hat at his side. "Well, I'm here to do the sorting."

"Conn—"

Shoving the hat back onto his head, he stepped around her bag on the stoop as he descended. Then he halted right next to her, and she went still, taking in the scent of him.

Hay and clover. It was as if he'd already become a part of her. A part that she had to let go.

"If it's the last thing I do," he said in a low voice, "I'm going to show you who I really am, Rita. Bet on that."

As he walked away, why did she get the impression that Conn Flannigan would be dogging every step she took from now on?

And, most disturbingly, why was her heart jumping at the very thought?

A couple of hours later, Rita stepped back, hand over her heart, as she surveyed her best friend in the long antique mirror that stood in the dressing room in back of the church. Violet's gown was just as polished as she was, with long sleeves and button detail, and a cut-out back with lace embellishments. A short veil was worked into her upswept red hair.

For a stolen second, Rita imagined that she wasn't wearing the latte-colored satin cocktail dress that allowed her enough room to barely disguise her growing belly. She imagined *she* was the bride.

And that a certain cowboy who'd stubbornly moseyed back into town would be waiting for her at the altar.

"Thinking about Conn?" Violet asked as she adjusted her décolletage.

Whoops. Bad maid of honor, *bad*.

"I'm thinking about how Davis is going to melt when he sees you walking down the aisle," Rita said. She meant it, too. Poor Davis was mincemeat.

Besides, this was Vi's wedding. It wasn't good timing for Rita to be thinking about how Conn made her weak in the knees or how she was dying to run outside after him just to make sure she hadn't imagined that he'd returned to St. Valentine yet again.

"You're not fooling anyone, you know." Violet turned away from the mirror, smiling. "You should've just asked him to come inside and watch the wedding."

"Yeah, that definitely would've shown him that I don't want him around."

"But you do."

Dang it. "Yeah. I do."

There were *those* words—"I do." And Rita couldn't help but wish yet again that things had turned out differently—that Conn had been the fantasy man she'd projected onto him that first night. That he'd lived up to all her wants and needs. That she might've been the one saying, "I do," someday if she would only open up to him.

But what was it Mom had always told her? "If dreams were dimes, I'd live in a sprawling mansion."

Speaking of moms, Violet's mother, Andrea, eased open the door, saying, "Knock, knock!"

"Come on in," Violet said.

Dressed in a tasteful, chocolate-hued long dress with her gray-and-red hair in a bun, Andrea closed the door behind her and sucked in a breath. "Oh, Vi. You're going to make me cry."

"No crying allowed." She turned around, fairly glowing. "This is the happiest day of my life."

Tears clogged Rita's throat. Darn those baby hormones.

After Andrea doted over her only child, she turned her attentions on Rita. It'd been that way for years, since Vi and Rita had grown up together. When Rita's parents had passed on, Andrea Osborne had taken their places in a lot of ways, offering a maternal shoulder to lean on when Rita needed it.

So it was no big surprise when Andrea noticed that something was wrong with Rita.

"It's Conn, isn't it?" she asked.

Rita shot Vi a glance, and Vi mouthed, "I didn't say a *word*."

"Is this all everyone in St. Valentine talks about?" Rita asked.

"Oh, honey, when a good-looker like that Conn Flannigan ambles into town, everyone talks." Andrea came over to link arms with Rita. "I got a good peek at him while you two were in the courtyard earlier. He can't seem to stay away from you, can he?"

Rita wanted to spill her guts to them, ask them if

she was being too willful and prideful. But, again, this was Vi's day.

"You're in a real spot," said Vi's mom, rubbing Rita's back.

"It's these crazy hormones pinging all around in me," Rita said.

Vi came over, too. "You're carrying his baby, Rita. That means you're attached to Conn in a significant way. He's always going to be a part of your life. There's no getting around that."

"I was attached to Kevin, too, and—"

Andrea put the kibosh on that. "You lived through what Kevin did, and you're going to come out of this with flying colors, too, because you've got a choice, Rita. You can sit here in your pretty dress and sob, or you can let go of the past and take a chance on the present."

Vi jumped right in. "And don't you dare say Conn left you a second time. You pretty much told him to take a hike. Kevin would've gone no matter what."

Andrea and Vi walked Rita to the mirror, and what Rita saw wasn't a bridesmaid who would never be a true, long-lasting bride—she saw that her friends might just be right.

She saw a woman with a growing baby bump in a gorgeous dress…and with a choice in what she wanted from the father.

"I know you're looking for a guarantee," Andrea said softly. "But there aren't any of those in life. There're just risks that we have to take to find happiness. You don't get one without the other."

Vi put her arm around Rita. "I took a risk with Davis, and here I am."

"Risks are…scary," Rita finally said. And it was the first time she'd been utterly honest with them. The words just seemed so naked, in need of being covered up.

But Vi and Andrea hugged her, as if they completely understood.

Andrea backed away, and Rita fully embraced Vi as tightly as she could. The music started up in the church. "Jesu, Joy of Man's Desiring." The song that would usher in the rest of Vi's life.

Time for the bride. Time for Vi and Davis's future to start.

"Just go out there and get him, would you?" Rita whispered in her friend's ear.

As Vi backed away with a radiant smile on her face, then headed for the door, Rita almost forgot that Conn had all but promised he was going to catch up to her sooner or later.

Almost.

Conn had frittered away the time by driving to the Co-Zee Inn on the east side of St. Valentine, checking in to it for the second time this month, and then catching up with the news on TV until he guessed the wedding was over. All the while, though, his thoughts were racing.

Could he really live up to *this* promise he'd made to Rita, unlike the one he'd made to her the morning after their night together, when he'd said he was going to come back and resume their romance? It seemed the most important thing in the world to prove to her that he was responsible now. Actually, it was important to him, too.

If it's the last thing I do, he'd said, *I'm going to show you who I really am.*

He hadn't come back to St. Valentine to uncover memories this time—he was here to build them. But these memories would be about the child he'd created during that one, life-changing night.

What about Rita, though?

His heart told him that, yes, he was here for her, too. That there was something between them that he hadn't quite grasped onto in his piecemeal memories. But, more important, every time he looked at her now, he couldn't look away. This morning, as she'd stood in front of him in sweats, her hair in curly, haphazard disarray, she'd been the most stunning woman in the world.

It was something chemical in him that bubbled every time he got close.

It was something he couldn't fight.

He just had to know what it was and why it wouldn't go away.

After he drove to town, he parked in a public dirt lot, then walked to Amati Street. The farther he strolled down the boardwalk, the more he could hear the music coming from the Queen of Hearts Saloon. He also caught a glimpse of fancied-up people hanging around outside, laughing and socializing.

The wedding reception.

Adrenaline fizzed in him as he came to the front of the timeworn building, where there was a crowd of gray-haired men smoking pipes with cherry-scented tobacco. An oldster who resembled a crazy-haired cowpoke wearing a wrinkled blue suit and a bolo that had gone askew busted out of the bar and grill, waving everyone inside.

"Bride and groom are on their way," he said. "Time to get in here for a toast!"

While he ushered the group into the saloon, Conn didn't move an inch.

"You, too," said the man, coming down the wooden steps, his hand extended. "There're no strangers in St. Valentine. I'm Wiley Scott, family friend."

Conn shook his hand. "Conn Flannigan. I'm afraid I don't really know the bride or groom. There's just a member of the wedding party that I…"

"Who?"

Oddly, Conn felt a rush of heat cover his face. "Rita Niles."

"You're in the proper place then. She looks right lovely, too, in that dress." Before going through the doorway again, Wiley waved Conn in. "Come on. Have a drink!"

But Conn merely watched the old man go. Rita was in there, and…

A stray, foreign thought punched through him. He still had time to hightail it back to the ranch in his truck.

He shook his head. Just where the hell had *that* come from?

Yet Conn didn't really need to ask. The thought had arrived so naturally that it had to have originated from habit, from years of thinking that way…and escaping from hard situations with women.

Was something inside of him preserving the bachelorhood that he had reportedly enjoyed so much?

He listened to the gaiety inside the saloon, seeing through the doorway how people were hugging and enjoying each other. In spite of himself, more unwelcome thoughts crowded him, convenient and easy.

If he went in there, would Rita make a scene at the mere sight of him? Would she say something like, *I thought you knew enough to leave me alone and just go home...*

Was that what he *wanted* her to say, just so he could assure himself that he'd given it the good old All-American try?

Again, it sounded like something the old Conn would've embraced.

An unfamiliar voice cut through everything else. "Looks like there're folks from different sides of town in there, having fun. Things have come a long way for this place lately."

Conn glanced to the other side of the doorway, where he hadn't noticed a man loitering. He was dressed in black, from his low-dipped cowboy hat to his boots. The only deviation in color was his silver belt buckle, which Conn recognized as a rodeo trophy.

Conn nodded to him, and for an instant, he thought that the man actually hadn't said anything at all. But then the guy used his knuckles to nudge up the brim of his hat so his dark eyes were visible.

"Jared." He had a hard face, chiseled, but it wasn't entirely unfriendly. Still, Conn got the feeling this guy wasn't terribly sociable.

Then he realized that Jared resembled the pictures of the infamous town founder, Tony Amati, that he'd seen in newspaper articles and even on TV. How about that.

"I'm Conn."

The man nodded, too, his gaze taking in Conn's casual wardrobe. "Looks like you weren't at the wedding. I wasn't, either, but I'm never one to miss a party."

"Even from the outside?"

Jared smiled. "I prefer it that way."

Conn had heard about the look-alike's standoffishness, and also that he wasn't being very cooperative in Violet and Davis Jackson's journalistic investigation into Tony Amati's long-ago life and death. But before he could say anything about it, his new pal wandered away, as if he'd never had any intention of being a part of the reception.

Conn just watched him go. It was almost like seeing a dark ghost walk away. He recognized ghosts, too, because that was how he'd felt so often recently—disassociated, alienated, on the fringes of so many things.

It didn't appeal in the slightest.

With a new sense of purpose, Conn walked through the Queen of Hearts' doors, looking past all the people to the only woman he wanted to find.

And as Rita locked gazes with him, the rest of the world and all its troubles ceased to exist, just as they seemingly had during their one night together.

So this is what it's like, Rita thought when Conn walked into the saloon.

This was how it felt to be looked at by that one special man, just as Davis had looked at Violet at the wedding ceremony, when she had appeared in her bridal gown and he hadn't been able to take his eyes off her.

Rita didn't remember ever feeling like this, even when she'd been engaged to Kevin. But that had been years ago, and so many ugly things had happened between them that it was hard to remember the good times, although Rita knew they had existed.

Now, as Conn smiled at her, fairy-tale dust seemed

to shimmer through her veins. Out of defensive instinct, she almost shut off the feeling, just as she always did.

But then she thought of the moment she had seen their baby on the monitor in the doctor's office, and when Dr. Ambrose had told her the child was a girl.

And how she'd wished Conn were there for all of it.

You can sit here in your pretty dress and sob, or you can let go of the past and take a chance on the present.

At the echo of Andrea's words from earlier in the day, Rita took that chance and smiled back at Conn across the room.

Maybe she wasn't altogether ready to offer her heart, but she could offer him an opportunity. He was the father of her baby, and he had seemed so genuine this morning, putting himself on the line and coming back here to see if they could work something out.

Conn deserved to at least make his case about the baby to her.

He started to thread through everyone in the room, which had been cleared for the reception, with the usual tables relegated to a rarely used adjoining room that was normally separated by a sliding door.

He never took his gaze from hers, and as he got closer, her heart beat louder...louder...

Until he was standing in front of her.

Her mouth was dry, but she worked up enough courage to say, "I'm glad you came."

Before he could answer, the room exploded in applause and cheers as the bride and groom entered. When they paused at the doorway, the wagon-wheel light fixtures lent illumination to Violet's joyous glow. Even a tuxedo-clad Davis, whose perpetually tossed dark blond hair was actually tamed for the wedding, looked as if he were walking on clouds.

Wiley Scott led the toast to the new couple, but Rita barely heard any of it. She couldn't stop thinking about the cowboy at her side.

This time, she wasn't imagining him being here, as she had during the sonogram. He had really come back again.

If only it was for more than an obligation, though...

The dancing started with a tried-and-true wedding tune, "Celebration." On the floor, everyone from the bride's and groom's relatives to townsfolk—some from mining families like Vi's, some from the rich side of town like Davis's—was having fun. Even Davis's hoity-toity, fashion-victim mom was on the outskirts, holding a drink and smiling as if she were trying very hard to enjoy herself as she watched her son and Violet posing for a picture.

When Rita saw that her daughter had pulled some of her little friends as well as her uncle Nick and her aunt Kim onto the floor, too, Rita waved at them. Kristy did a cute rear-end-wiggling shimmy in her flower-girl dress while Kim, who'd been watching her during the wedding, got to a knee to plant a kiss on her niece's cheek.

Conn bent to Rita's ear so she could hear him over the music. "You look beautiful."

And...melting again. She felt as if she'd been left too long in the sun.

"Thanks." Was she blushing now, too?

Why did he have that power over her when no one else could outwardly faze her?

She gestured toward his cowboy hat, Western shirt and jeans. "You look…"

"Like I wasn't invited?" he asked, laughing.

"I invited you."

Her blush intensified. Was she actually doing something like flirting?

Uh-uh. She was willing to give him the chance to show her that he was more than a fly-by-night playboy and that he had it in him to be a dad, but here she was, stepping over a line she shouldn't be crossing on a personal level.

Couldn't happen.

But he didn't make an issue out of it. And soon, when the music flowed into another song—"Life's a Dance," a tune she hadn't heard in a long, long time—Conn took her hand without even asking, leading her onto the dance floor.

Her first impulse was to resist, but she didn't. Couldn't. Truthfully, it didn't take but a moment for them to ease right into the rotation of other dancers as they two-stepped and circled the floor.

She felt the burn of judgment singeing her from the observers they were passing. Margery Wilmore from the hotel, who'd always clucked her tongue at Rita and monitored every move she made. A few miners' wives from a knitting circle who met in the saloon—part of the moral majority in this town.

But then Conn danced her past Vi's mom, and Rita met her optimistic gaze.

When Andrea gave Rita a subtle wink, Rita smiled, then turned her full attention on Conn.

His laughing blue eyes, his playful grin… She didn't care if the whole town would gossip about her and speculate if he was the dad of her new baby. Lost in his gaze, she couldn't care less, because he was all that existed in this instant.

But all too soon, the song ended, and they didn't let go of each other. She could feel her pulse flitting over every inch of her skin.

What next? she thought.

As she anticipated the answer, Conn smiled at her, and once again, he became her fantasy man, even though she knew the dream would probably end all too quickly.

Chapter Six

The tension was almost strong enough to be bullet-proof, and Rita couldn't stand a moment more of waiting as she looked at Conn and he looked at her.

Seconds languished.

Heat surrounded them.

"I could use something to drink," she said finally.

Yup. Leave it to her to ruin a moment.

At first, he seemed stymied. But then he laughed, slowly letting her go, much to her relief.

"I'll get us something," he said.

As a fast song started up, he made his way toward the bar, coming back with two lemonades with mint sprigs decorating the rims. Then he jerked his chin toward the quieter side room, silently asking if she wanted to go in there.

They found an empty table toward the back, and

after he set down the drinks, he pulled out a chair for her to sit.

After she did, he said, "I know you've got a spot at the bridal-party table, but I thought you might like a break from some of the noise."

"You just want to show me that you're responsible, right?" she asked.

He shrugged good-naturedly, then took a seat next to her. The awkwardness of their situation still loomed, but she didn't want it to settle. Not when it seemed so simple right now to remember why they'd gotten together that one night. Every awful thing that had come afterward didn't seem to matter as much while they were in this secluded space, away from everyone else.

When she rubbed her palm over her tummy—a gesture that had become a soothing habit—she caught him watching.

Did he want to feel the bump? It sure looked like it.

Again, she thought of the sonogram, and how she'd wished for him to see it, too.

It was clear that he sensed her confusion. "You're scared to death that I'm going to treat you like your ex-fiancé did, aren't you?"

She didn't know what to say at his bluntness.

"Don't be afraid." He leaned forward in his chair, his hands clasped.

She noticed how strong they were, work-roughened, and her pulse skipped.

"Rita, you can trust me. And don't say that I can't be sure of that because I have no past to base that on. I know it deep down."

She nodded. "Okay."

"You say that as if you're still not sure." He sat back in his chair. "Hell, I suppose I can't blame you."

He pushed his hat back on his head, and his face just about broke her heart all over again. It wasn't just that he was as handsome as the devil—there was *something* about him that got to her, reaching inside and twisting.

"You weren't my first affair on the road," he said. "My brothers tell me that I was pretty good at playing the field, that I didn't stay in one woman's arms for long."

There it went again—a needling ache in her chest. But how could she have ever thought that she was the first for him?

"You never had a long-term girlfriend?" she asked.

"Not even close, as far as I understand. But after I got out of the hospital, I tried to find out if my brothers were wrong. I dug through old pictures, looked through my email accounts, but there wasn't one photo of a woman, and there weren't any messages or love letters showing that I had some kind of relationship waiting in the wings—or that I even had a significant one in the past. And I didn't have any phone numbers for women outside of business stored in my phone."

Rita's heart was sinking with every word. "What makes you think you won't go back to being that way?"

"Because I don't feel like the same man I keep hearing about," he said, his voice firm.

Rita surveyed Conn, but there was nothing duplicitous about him. What would he have to gain by coming back here?

And why did she keep having to doubt his word?

"So you're telling me that you've come here to change your life?" she asked.

"Yeah. What if this is the man I'm meant to be?"

He sounded so damned full of conviction that it wrung her out.

"I'm going to live up to whatever a baby would need, Rita," he said. "My ranch isn't so far away that I couldn't be here for him or her."

He was making a commitment—or at least the best one he could manage on this tenuous ground.

Should she offer as much back to him, tell him that she was carrying a girl?

No. That wasn't a step she was prepared to take. Not just yet. It seemed too much to give up too soon.

"Are you talking about visitation rights?" she asked.

"I'm not getting into legal stuff. I just want to be an important part of this child's life."

Just the thought of losing this baby to a half-baked custody arrangement made her nerves flail.

Damn him. Damn her, too, for not being able to trust him.

Nipped by panic, she fought to distance herself from him, to see if he would change his mind about coming on so strong if she showed him that it wasn't working with her. "Is this all about proving this 'new man' theory to yourself, Conn?"

He kept his silence.

"I mean," she said, "you're not losing sight of what it really means to be a dad in all this, are you? Fatherhood's not a part-time deal. A child takes everything you have to give—your heart, soul and more time than a human actually has at their disposal."

He was already shaking his head. "Just stop right there. Clearly, I'm not doing a good job of saying what I really want to say to you."

"Which is…?"

"That I came here to win you over, Rita. About the baby and…"

As he trailed off, a shock jolted her.

"And what?" she asked.

He bent forward, taking her hand again, just as if he was about to lead her out of the room and onto the floor for another dance.

A dance she didn't know the steps to, but wanted so badly to learn, if only she could allow herself to.

"Rita?"

At the sound of the female voice, Rita dragged her glance away from Conn. She saw her sister, Kim, who was uncomfortably garbed in an ill-fitting floral skirt and blouse paired with her Resistol hat and Justin boots. She made her way through the other tables, which were still basically empty because of the dancing in the bigger room.

"Here you are," she said. "You're the only one missing at the wedding party's table."

"I'll be right there," Rita said as Kim gave Conn an arch look, then left.

Conn rose to his feet, extending a hand to help Rita out of her chair. "Maybe you could just take a drive with me after the wedding. A short one."

She looked at his offered hand. Taking a drive would be the first real step into something beyond a mere tap dance around the true issues between them. Taking a drive would mean taking a risk.

Once more, she saw a flash of her little baby's sonogram.

With a held breath, Rita grasped on to his hand, and he pulled her gently to her feet.

"Where are we going?" she asked.

Here they were again, Conn on one side of a truck cab and Rita on the other with the radio playing a soft tune as the late-afternoon scenery rolled by.

But unlike the time he'd taken her to the fish shack, it was his own truck he was driving today, and things were somewhat less awkward between them, now that they'd cleared a bit of air back at the wedding.

That wasn't to say all their issues were taken care of. It was obvious that Rita still didn't trust him as far as she could throw him.

Yet could he fault her for that? She'd been crushed before by a jerk who'd left her to raise a child alone. The past was repeating itself for Rita, and it would take a lot of winning over for Conn to persuade her that he wasn't going to be the same as her ex.

A tweak of conscience got to him as he wondered if, maybe, he might turn out to be a whole lot more like him than he would like.

He turned off the main road near the Heartland condominium complex, where he'd heard Tony Amati used to have a ranch before it was torn down for the sake of modern progress.

"Are we going where I think we are?" Rita asked.

She didn't sound put out that he'd kept her guessing ever since they'd left the reception. In fact, she smiled at him, looking every bit as breathtaking as she had earlier, when he'd first seen her across the saloon in her creamed-coffee-colored dress and with her hair arranged in a bundle of curls, just as if she were at some old-time ball. Honestly, Conn thought she'd been just as appealing—sexier, even—this morning in those sweats that clung to her curves, but he couldn't stop gazing at her either way.

"And where do you think we're going?" he asked, guiding the truck toward a copse of pines off the country lane.

"Lookout Point."

"We'll see if you're right about that soon enough."

He pulled the truck into a spot near some flat rocks, cut the engine, then went around to her side. After opening the door, he aided her in getting out. This dress showcased her belly, and he was itching to put his hand on the curve of it.

Was that weird, or did it just mean he was father material?

"I thought," he said, "that this might be a peaceful place to talk, away from any ears."

Since the November weather still hadn't turned cold, she had brought a thin, sheer wrap, and she wound it around her. "Do you know the stories about this place?"

"I've heard a few rumblings in town, that's why it caught my attention. There's something about how Tony Amati used to come to this very spot when he got here in the 1920s, and he would look down on the land that would hold his town someday. He used to picture it, dream about it, until it came to fruition."

They started walking through the trees, their shoes crunching over pine needles, toward a place where the branches opened up over a mild drop-off where you could see St. Valentine down below in the near distance. The white church seemed to gleam in the center of the old part of town while, on the east side, mansions and pools waned under the softening gaze of the sun.

Rita took a seat on a rock that boasted a flat surface, as if it'd been sat on so many times that it had been shaped for just such a thing.

Except Conn noticed there was room for two.

"They also call this Heartbreak Hill," Rita said, hugging her wrap around herself. "Supposedly, there were doomed lovers who used to meet here."

Was she giving him some kind of warning? "Who were they?"

"The old-timers will tell you it's the same couple who haunts my hotel. If you believe the stories."

Conn leaned his shoulder against a tree. "Sounds as if you know a few of those stories, seeing as it's your hotel."

"Oh, they're mostly legends. The couple consisted of a gentleman passing through town on his way west to seek a better future and a good-time girl who liked her booze and boys. They got caught by her husband and gunned down."

"So those are your resident ghosts?"

"Right. Every once in a while, we'll get some nervous Nellies who come in and tell tales about spirits materializing by their bed or touching their shoulder while they were shaving. Funny thing is, though, that it's never in the room where the deaths supposedly occurred. But it's good for business. It draws in the curious, especially nowadays with the Tony Amati story."

Conn chuckled. "If I'd known this was a spot for the doomed, I would've kept away from here."

Rita paused, then hugged herself even tighter. "I'm hoping our doomed phase has passed, Conn."

What exactly did that mean? They'd had such a bumpy conversation at the wedding that he wasn't sure just where he stood with her right now. That's why he'd wanted to talk to her afterward, for some clarification.

All he knew for sure was that he'd meant every word he'd said to her about being the man he felt he was today. It was as if he'd been born to say such things to her, to make such promises about being responsible.

And when she'd asked if he was overlooking the reality of truly being a father, he'd at first been taken aback, wondering if she had a point.

Was the baby quite real to him yet? Or was he chasing some dream?

His gaze strayed to her again, as it inevitably did, time after time. Without even planning to, he took a step closer to her. "What's it going to take to win you over, Rita?"

A hitch of breath, a quick look. "Win me over?"

"That's right, because the more I'm around you, the more I wonder what that night truly meant to me. I feel like I was really going to come back for a second night with you, you know." He didn't add that he wasn't sure how long he would've stayed. Because, with the way he was feeling now, it could've been forever.

If he could depend on his gut instinct.

Her eyes were pools of gray, glassy with a wariness that he would do anything to vanquish. "I just don't know how far to trust you. Or…me."

"That's understandable." He came a step closer.

"I'm not even sure where to start."

"You started by saying yes a few times today. Dancing with me, coming out here with me, introducing me to Violet when you went to the wedding table…"

It hadn't been a long greeting, but it had meant something to him. An acceptance of sorts, as small as it was.

"I don't know how many yeses will get me in trouble," Rita said. "It seems that they always do."

He bent to a knee by the rock. "The trouble has to end sometime. And it sounds to me like you have the talent to turn a tough situation into something good, like you did with Kristy."

Rita sighed as the sky blushed to orange over a darker blue.

"Maybe it's just a matter of us spending more time together," she said. "Getting to know each other, since you're so hell-bent on sticking around."

"I'd like that."

"Would you?" She gave him a challenging look. "Then there's an event tomorrow at the high school. The Chamber of Commerce sponsors a lunch for a lot of natural-gas field employees coming home for Thanksgiving week."

She'd snagged a bit on the last part, and he guessed it might be because her ex had been one of those employees who'd returned from the fields at this time of the year.

She composed herself. "In the past, more than a few employees would save vacation time to come home, and for the past few years the town has thrown this lunch to promote a sense of community. Not that there was ever much of one before."

"What happened to change that this year?"

"Davis Jackson's attempts to strengthen the economy are finally paying off. And Violet's done a lot to help, especially when it comes to promoting St. Valentine with the Tony Amati story. I think people saw that if a guy from the rich part of town and a miner's girl could come together, everyone else should give it a shot, too."

"Well, you can count me in for that lunch," he said.

"Even if they ask you to serve tables?"

He lifted an eyebrow.

She shrugged. "I'm a volunteer, since I'm a member of the Chamber of Commerce, so you might get pressed into service, too."

"It won't be a problem."

It seemed as if he'd said just the right thing to her. She gazed at him, then smiled, absently resting a hand on her tummy, as he noticed she often did.

He watched her, imagining…

As if in surrender, she took him by the hand. "Jeez, you're killing me. Here."

When she placed his palm on her belly, saying "yes" to him yet another time today, his world expanded with the force of a bursting heartbeat.

God, this felt good, and he couldn't say exactly why. Maybe it was more intimate than he ever remembered being with anyone. Maybe it was because he could picture the baby inside, a child who already had his eyes, his nose.

Now, more than ever, as he imagined everything else about this child, he knew he'd made the right choice in coming back to St. Valentine.

He just had to make sure Rita came to realize it, too.

On the way home, Rita felt a hum of awareness between her and Conn, almost as if it were some sort of force field that was rising up from the truck's seat. It didn't help that the buzz of tires on the road filled her head, adding to the illusion.

But hadn't most of the day been something like a dream? Him showing up at the church this morning, then the reception, then the both of them going to Heart-break Hill, where she'd let him touch her baby bump?

She wasn't sure what it was about Conn that made her act so impulsively sometimes. When she had seen him looking at how she was rubbing the slight mound of her tummy under her bridesmaid's dress, her blood had shot straight to her heart, and she had thought, *What would be the harm in just indulging him for a second?*

And she had brought his hand over to her stomach, holding back a long, sharp sigh as the imprint of his fingers, his palm, seeped into her.

After that, she had played the moment off, laughing awkwardly, telling him that the baby would be happy that he had said his first hello. All the while, Conn had smiled, as if Rita had given him something that he would never get again—or had *ever* gotten.

Not that he would know that for certain, though.

They were approaching Piell's Gas Station on the road into town, with its old Phillips 66 and Pumps Are Open signs lit under the fallen night.

"Mind if I stop?" Conn asked. "My tank could use some gas."

"Fine with me."

Stopping would give her a breather from that electri-fied force field that was still trying to pull her closer to him, so she was all for it. But as he stopped the truck, climbed out and went inside to pre-pay for the gas, she didn't get a break of any kind—not as she watched the way he ambled toward the convenience store, the way his jeans molded to his legs, his slim hips flaring up to a broad back and wide shoulders under his blue shirt.

Once upon a time, she had pressed her bare chest against that back, luxuriating in the feel of her breasts against corded muscle and smooth skin. It had been a long time since she had been that close to a man. Her, a woman who had been intimate with only one other guy her entire life.

But she had known that Conn was *it* for her in that moment.

Had she been so wrong?

Pushing away the question—she knew better than to give in to him again—she blew out a breath, grabbing the beaded clutch she had brought to the wedding so she could put a coat of lip balm on. Then she got a glimpse of her phone screen, and she saw that she had missed a text from Violet.

Disappeared with Conn just as soon as you could, didn't you? :)

It had come through about an hour ago, when Rita had been on Heartbreak Hill with Conn. She texted back.

Aren't you supposed to be going on a honeymoon?

Violet must've had her phone handy, because Rita's rang. Leave it to a reporter to jump on a breaking story.

"We're leaving for the airport in a half hour," Vi said just as soon as Rita answered. "So that gives me time to bug you."

"I can't talk long." Rita could see Conn through the window of the convenience store. Ori Piell, who had his Pennzoil cap on backward, was talking Conn's ear off, and Conn's manners were obviously too good to cut the bearded man's conversation short.

Rita added, "If you're calling to make sure I haven't done anything stupid with Conn yet, you're in luck. I'm holding strong."

"I'm impressed. He's cute, Rita."

She glowed with something like blushing agreement. "In spite of all the baggage, you mean."

"He seemed to be keeping everything together when I met him at the wedding."

"That's because Conn is as charming as they come. I can tell you firsthand that he's able to make a girl believe anything he wants her to."

Rita frowned at her own words. Was that what was happening with him now? Was she falling into a "Conn trap," snagged by his charm for the moment and setting herself up for a fall in the end?

"Well," Vi said. "I'm just altogether impressed that you're dealing with this head-on."

"I've only yet begun to deal. Kristy's going to be real curious about him, and I'm not sure how to approach *that* whole scenario yet."

"Because she's never really had a man in her life, and Conn's the first one who's going to be in it."

"Wait—I don't know how much he's going to be a part of my life. It's too soon to tell. We still have to work out the details about how this baby will be raised." *If* he stayed the course with all the promises he was making.

Vi apparently heard the doubt in Rita's tone. "You'll figure it out. You always do."

"Thanks. But in the meantime, I've got to think of a way to keep Kristy from getting her hopes up when she sees me spending time with Conn. She's already giving him puppy-eyed looks, like she's measuring him up."

He was coming out of the convenience store, and Rita quelled a blip of adrenaline that shocked her through and through.

"I should go," she said as he got to the truck and started to put gas in the tank. "And you should, too, Mrs. Jackson."

Vi and Davis had planned to stay in a few Scottish castles as they explored the country for the next week and a half. What a life.

"Mrs. Jackson," Vi said with a sigh. "I used to secretly write that all over my high school notebooks when Davis and I were kids. Now it's real."

"Lucky." Rita smiled, happy that her friend's dreams had come true. "Travel safe, and say hi to the groom."

"Will do. And Rita?"

"You don't have to say anything more about sucking it up and taking a chance." Rita watched Conn in the sideview mirror. "I'm taking more of them than I ever imagined."

They said goodbye, and soon, Conn was done, getting into the truck and tipping back his hat on his head.

"That Ori fellow?" he said, motioning toward the convenience store. "Nice as can be, but he could talk a donkey's hind leg off."

Rita laughed. She hadn't expected much humor tonight, but sometimes Conn had a way about him.

He started the truck up. "Sorry it took me longer than it should've."

"No sorries required."

He drove the short distance back to her hotel, where a hint of stars twinkled in the night sky. He pulled up in front of the boardwalk, then insisted on opening the passenger-side door for her, reaching out a hand to help her to the ground.

The gesture was so gentlemanly, especially with her in this long satin dress, that Rita almost felt as if some old-fashioned courting was going on.

And, God help her, she liked it.

When he started to bring her to the empty boardwalk and the front door, Rita stopped him.

This wasn't a date, after all.

"It was nice to get a few things in order," she said.

"It was a start."

Conn was so tall that she had to look up at him. His height—and his wiry strength—made her pulse flutter.

She cleared her throat. "I'll see you tomorrow afternoon at the high school gym for the Chamber of Commerce lunch then?"

"Definitely." He said it again, as if he was determined to show her just how reliable he could be.

That should've been the capper on the night, yet, for some reason, she wasn't going anywhere. It was as if he still had a pull on her—that magnetic force that wouldn't allow her to leave.

As she looked up at him again, she lingered on the shape of his mouth. She had said yes to him several times today, so what if she just leaned in a little closer…?

It seemed as if he were thinking the same thing, because he came a bit nearer, close enough so that she could hear him breathing.

And every breath made her go a little weaker.

But then, as if he remembered why he was here—to

prove that he was more than that scattered playboy—he backed away toward the truck.

"'Night, Rita," he said.

She blinked, her skin heating.

Had that just been her, inviting a kiss?

"'Night, Conn," she said quickly. Then she climbed the couple of steps leading up to the boardwalk, wanting to get inside as soon as possible.

Yet she couldn't stop herself from glancing back at him, finding him still standing there by his truck, as if he didn't want to go anywhere, either.

Rita opened the lobby door and shut it firmly behind her, before she could change her mind and say yes to him one too many times.

Chapter Seven

"When is Mr. Conn coming?" Kristy asked as she held Rita's hand on the way into St. Valentine High School.

"He might already be here." Rita had to tread lightly as far as her daughter was concerned. At four years old, Kristy had never been around men much on a personal level, except for her uncle Nick. One of Rita's biggest fears was that Kristy might be so hungry for a father figure that she would attach too easily to any man Rita brought home.

As they walked through the high school's brick lobby, the musty smell of days gone by got to Rita. This was where she had laid her head on Kevin's shoulder while they sat on the benches before school. This was where she'd thought she'd fallen in love.

Kristy pulled Rita out of her painfully nostalgic fog

by tugging on her hand, then yanking her into the gym, which was empty, since they were early for the Chamber of Commerce lunch.

"Come on, Mommy!"

"I'm right behind you." And her stomach was gnarled in knots, anticipating Conn waiting for them.

At first, when they entered the gym, Rita only saw row upon row of linen-covered tables set with heavy paper plates, plastic silverware and ruffled turkey centerpieces that the high school Future Homemakers of America club had already put out.

Kristy stood in the center of it all in her red velvet dress and tights, her hands on her hips as she peered around for Conn, disappointment written all over her face.

Rita's chest clenched. If Kristy had been old enough, this was what she might've looked like on the night her father had left, if she had come into a room and tried to find him.

"He's just not here yet," Rita said, going to Kristy and giving her a big kiss on the forehead.

But then she heard a voice echoing off the gym's walls.

"Who's not here?"

Conn. And as Rita and Kristy spun around to see him, Rita wanted to run over, throw her arms around him and thank him for keeping his word.

Sure, this was only a casual meeting but… Well, it was more than that, too. More than Rita was used to from men.

Kristy chose that moment to turn into a shy girl, and she pressed against Rita's leg, holding on to her wool skirt with one hand.

As Rita fought the blush she knew was consuming her face, she played off her excitement. "A man who isn't afraid of a little work. Glad you showed up."

"Wouldn't miss it." His boots thudded on the gym floor as he sauntered the rest of the way to them. "Morning, Kristy."

She gave him a slight wave before doubling her efforts to cling to Rita.

"Who *are* you?" Rita said to her normally outgoing daughter, laughing.

Conn grinned at Kristy. "Are you going to help us serve the food?"

"I'm helping Mommy."

Rita ruffled her curls just as a couple of women walked into the gym with their children.

They waved to Rita, and Kristy gave a little hop at the sight of the other children.

"Can I go play?" she whispered loudly.

The other kids had already sprinted over to a set of wooden bleachers that had been pulled out from the wall, creating a lounging area. Any minute, some volunteer students from the Future Homemakers were scheduled to begin babysitting duty.

"Sure you can," Rita said to Kristy. "But don't climb past the second step, okay?"

"Okay!" Kristy was already off and running.

Rita greeted the other girls' mothers. They said hi back, then gave Conn a subtle once-over as they made their way toward the door near the stage, where the volunteers would be congregating. Apparently, they thought it best to give Rita time alone with this new man who was still a stranger to everyone else.

But Conn didn't seem to mind. He was smiling and

watching Kristy fuss over a rag doll that one of the other girls had brought.

"She's a carbon copy of you," Conn said.

"Hopefully the new and improved version."

Rita was just joking, but Conn looked at her with a brow cocked.

"I wasn't thinking there was room for improvement," he said, and just those couple of words sent a tumble of shivers through her.

The charmer, she thought. The same man who had wrapped her around his finger that first night.

But he *was* here, with her, in spite of all the odds.

More people had come through the doors, saying hi to Rita and Conn, then going toward the stage door. The Future Homemaker teen volunteers arrived, checking in with Rita before taking Kristy and the other kids to the playroom where the high school's child-development class held a nursery school during the week.

Kristy rushed to Rita for a hug before she left. "Bye, Mom."

"I'll see you when they bring you back to serve the food," she said.

But Kristy wasn't finished, and Rita got the feeling that her daughter was showing off for Conn. "See you later, alligator."

"After a while, crocodile."

The exchange always tickled Kristy's funny bone, and she giggled just before she leaped over to Conn, waving at him up close and personal before taking off with the others.

Rita could tell that he was utterly charmed by her daughter as they went to the staging area, and it made her proud that she had raised such a girl.

And happier than she had been in a long time.

As she risked one more glance at him, she wondered if he was thinking of their own child and how *she* would grow up.

If he only knew their baby was a she…

Rita sighed. Someday soon, if everything went well, she would tell Conn everything.

Someday.

Backstage, the main organizers of the function, Jennifer Neeson and Lianna Hurst, were handing out flyers with directions for each volunteer job.

"I brought another victim," Rita said to Jennifer, whose long, lustrous dark hair was in a sleek ponytail. She was wearing a tight yellow cashmere sweater dress, hardly an outfit meant for food service.

Jennifer looked Conn up and down, and Rita's claws almost came out. The woman was probably the most aggressive bachelorette in St. Valentine.

Then Ms. Maneater smiled at Conn, as if proving Rita's fears. "New additions are *always* welcome."

Even the way she gave him a flyer was suggestive.

Conn merely nodded to her and started reading his sheet. He didn't even give Jennifer a second look, and honestly, Rita was watching very closely to see if he would.

Was the playboy in there somewhere?

Jennifer pouted ever so slightly before just about shoving Rita's own flyer toward her.

Years of having to deal with Jennifer Neeson and her fake high school laugh—as well as the way she used to flirt with Kevin during English class—brought the devil out in Rita. So she laid her hand on Conn's arm and guided him to the wings.

But Conn wasn't a fool. When they were alone, he raised his gaze from his sheet of paper, a grin swiping his mouth.

"Don't tell me," he said. "She's your second best friend after Violet."

"Hah-hah. Jennifer Neeson doesn't even have the sense to leave the cashmere at home during a hash-slinging event." Rita rolled her eyes. "What am I saying? She probably has carpets made of cashmere. She's the mayor's daughter and hasn't lived a day when she wasn't privileged. If she gets a spot on her sweater, she'll just toss it in the trash."

Conn smiled, but his gaze drifted to his arm where she was touching him. Slowly, Rita removed her hand. She hadn't realized she'd still been staking out her territory like that.

But it'd felt natural, as if touching him shouldn't be a big deal.

Much to her delight, he gave her a look that told her she could touch him anytime she wanted to.

"At any rate," Rita said, trying to recover from the blast of heat that had just fired through her, "Jennifer Neeson is *Violet's* archenemy. The rich girl versus the miner's daughter. It's been that way since school."

"Sounds like a lot of things pretty much stay the same in St. Valentine."

"Until they *don't* stay the same."

But she didn't add that it felt as if *she* were changing. Minute by minute, day by day, Conn seemed to be turning things around with her, and it was becoming easier to give in to change. And him.

Just then, Margery Wilmore, Rita's hotel employee who was handling the serving corps, beckoned the servers to another part of the backstage room. Grateful for the interruption, Rita went to her, standing next to Conn, ignoring how her skin came alive while she listened to Margery elaborate on their serving tasks.

He didn't have to be here, Rita thought all the while.

And yet…here he was, even when her ex-fiancé had turned to another woman and another life. For so many years, Rita had felt discarded, and it was hard to accept that maybe she was worthwhile to someone.

Especially this someone, who might end up changing his mind about her all too soon.

"By now," Margery said, concluding her speech, "the hosts should've begun seating everyone. So suit up!"

She pointed to a pile of aprons that had been donated by the Chamber of Commerce.

As everyone shuffled toward the serving gear, Conn winked down at Rita. "I've got 'em."

When he left her, Margery took his place next to Rita. The older woman had already put on her apron, which had a turkey shaped out of the words "St. Valentine" on it. Her plump chest made the bird's feathers spread out.

"Busy times, Rita?" she asked.

This was Margery's preamble to a friendly examination of Conn. Rita could predict it to a T.

"Holidays are always hectic," she said. "Luckily, we'll get a bit of a break at the hotel." This time of year was historically slow, and the bookings told Rita that this season would be no different, Tony Amati story or not.

"Hectic is the word, all right," Margery said. "I covered for you at the hotel after the reception yesterday because of your schedule." It would've sounded like chiding from anyone else, but Margery had a way of sweetly disguising it so you weren't quite certain. "I should've really stayed behind and played manager again today while you're here."

Total guilt trip. "We've got a lot of capable staff who know the ins and outs of the hotel, Margery. Besides, I'll be going in later."

"Honey, you've got to mind your condition." Taking a different tack, she gave a pointed look to Rita's belly. "You never told me you were pregnant."

The little dickens in Rita wanted so badly to tell Margery that she had merely put on some weight. Wouldn't that make her squirm?

But she was proud of this baby, just as she was about Kristy.

And proud of Conn?

No, she wouldn't be announcing that he was the father. It was way too soon.

Rita chose the path of least resistance, smiling at Margery and making the woman wonder about the details of the baby. But she did pat her on the arm to soften her refusal to elaborate. Truthfully, she didn't dislike Margery—she just didn't need the constant watchful eyes and clucking tongue.

She left Margery behind and went to Conn, who had two aprons in hand as he chatted with Aaron Rhodes, the scraggly-haired carpenter and Chamber of Commerce president.

"Rita," Aaron said, his green eyes amused as he greeted her. "Conn was just agreeing with me that men shouldn't wear turkey aprons."

Conn chuckled, gesturing to his ultra-manly gray Western shirt. "I don't mind getting dirty."

"Seconded," Aaron said.

"Come on." Rita stood on her tiptoes, snatching Conn's hat from his head and leaving his hair a dark, thick mess. "Be a sport."

She grabbed one of the aprons he was holding and hooked it over his head.

Aaron, who was just as much of a bachelor as Conn, laughed and walked away, shaking his head.

Conn glanced down at his apron-ized self. "I'm just going to keep repeating that this isn't so bad."

"It actually works on you, Conn," Rita said.

Well, *that* had just popped out. But it was true. Conn made apron-wearing kind of sexy, especially with his hair as disheveled as it was.

She remembered that night with him—her fingers combing through his hair, mussing it while he kissed her...

This had to stop. "I meant," she said, "that male chefs wear aprons. It's not like this one is made of lace and frills, anyway."

His smile quirked to the side. "You're telling me that it's a masculine apron."

"*Very* masculine."

And there she went again.

A fraught beat passed between them—one filled with a night of steamy kisses and caresses.

Was he thinking about the same thing?

Rita gave him back his hat, ending the moment. How did he manage to get the air around her so thick with suggestion?

Thankfully, it was time to serve, and after they washed up and Kristy joined Rita backstage, they went to the food carts that had been transferred from the

state-of-the-art culinary classroom that had been donated by Vi's new millionaire husband, Davis Jackson.

Rita lost Conn as they started their work in earnest,
grabbing prime rib–laden plates and entering the gym,
where everyone from old miners to town businessmen
sat at the tables, chatting festively.

Everybody, from every walk of St. Valentine life,
all in one room. Who would have ever guessed it could
happen?

But, in a corner of the gym, banded together, there
was a table of natural-gas-field guys. Most of them
were ex-kaolin miners who'd taken jobs a good distance away from their families in St. Valentine after
the mine closure.

Home for the holidays, Rita thought. And as she
watched them, she saw that a few were giving everyone
else in the room sullen glances, as if they didn't like
how the older ex-miners had evidently let bygones be
bygones and forgotten about how the mine closure had
left them high and dry.

Kristy poked Rita's leg. "Mommy, can I go play
again?"

They had made two food runs, and people had been
fussing over Kristy in her velvet dress and curls, an
activity that had obviously gotten old for her already.

There were a few Future Homemakers babysitters
near the bleachers, ready to escort kids who got tired
of serving to the classroom.

"Go ahead," Rita said.

Kristy sprinted away, and Rita went back for more
plates.

And wouldn't you know? As luck would have it, she
was assigned to go to the natural-gas employee table.

When she brought their food, a few guys recognized her, which she'd entirely expected since she'd gone to high school with most of them. More important, Kevin had worked by their sides in the fields before moving out of state with his newer lady love—one whom Rita wasn't even sure he'd ever married.

"Rita," said one of the men. Gene Farraday, who'd dressed for the occasion in a grubby baseball cap and hunting jacket. "How's Kevin doing?"

She froze, because everyone here knew damned well what had gone down with her ex-fiancé.

Someone snickered, but she didn't acknowledge him.

"I haven't heard from Kevin in a while," she replied.

Her calm answer only seemed to encourage Gene. "At first, I thought he might've made a home visit. Or does he even know that you've got a bun in the oven?"

Embarrassment burned her. Across the table, a frowning Wiley Scott was standing with a couple of plates in hand. He'd walked the social line between the miners and the richies for years as the town's former newspaper owner.

He set down his plates with a clatter in front of one of the workers.

"Watch yourself, Gene," he said, and it was the first time Rita had ever seen the normally carefree man angry.

Gene chuffed.

Wiley raised a finger. "We've all been getting along pretty well here while you've been off at work. Don't ruin that."

"Well, kumbaya." Gene made a prayer gesture, and it got a good laugh from his tablemates.

That's when she felt another presence at her side, and she didn't have to look to see who it was.

"How's it going here?" Conn asked in a low voice.

Gene gave him the stink-eye, but Conn didn't flinch as he returned it.

Rita didn't like where this was going, and she led Conn away just as Aaron Rhodes appeared, muttering to Gene in a firm and even tone. Gene rose from his seat with a cat-ate-the-canary grin to his friends and went with Aaron out of the gym.

Conn brought Rita back to the staging area, where they were alone. "Who was that?"

"Just a hell-raiser who used to work with my ex, Kevin. This is the first time someone has given me such blatant scorn since my belly started to show." Now that she was away from the crowd, she started to quiver with pent-up frustration. "I'm just happy that Kristy didn't see any of it."

Without another word, Conn wrapped her in his arms. "It's done, Rita. Nobody's going to give you that kind of bull anymore. I promise."

Yet another vow from Conn.

But as she sank into him, pressing her face against his chest, she believed it with her whole heart for as long as she could.

After Conn had made sure Rita was okay, he had taken her and Kristy to their Chevy, where Rita had tucked the little girl into her car seat and then lingered outside, where the sun was providing another warm day.

"It's nap time for her," Rita said. "And I should be getting back to the hotel, anyway."

"Sure." He wanted the day to be longer, to stretch

into the night. It didn't have to end with the ugliness he'd seen inside the gym when he could make things so much better for her.

It looked as if Rita was going to add something else, and Conn had the feeling it had something to do with "the incident" he'd cut into in the gym. But she just shrugged instead, putting her fingers on the car door handle.

Then she evidently changed her mind. "We've got a couple of rooms available in the hotel."

Okay. She hadn't said anything about that creep in the gymnasium, but Conn wondered if this was her way of reaching out and thanking him for backing her up.

"I guess," he said, "that I could use a change of scenery from the Co-Zee Inn. It doesn't have the kind of character I usually demand."

"My place has got character to spare. Just ask the ghosts." She smiled. "And you won't be charged a penny."

"Thanks, Rita, but no."

"*Yes.* You're my guest."

She was dancing around the real subject. He wasn't here on vacation, he was here for Rita and the baby, and when she put it that way, it seemed rude to deny her hospitality.

"I'll pack my stuff up and be there tomorrow," he said.

"Excellent. But I was thinking that maybe you'd want a good home-cooked meal tonight?"

Was this another "yes" from Rita? He would be a donkey to turn her down.

"Sounds perfect," he said. "But I'll tell you what.

You let me do the grunt work. You've been on your feet all day."

"It's no problem. I can—"

"Rita, when are you going to stop being Wonder Woman? You're pregnant, remember?"

Her gaze went so soft that something seemed to sigh in him.

"Are you coddling me, Conn?"

"I believe they call it pampering. And you need it."

After all, how many people did Rita have who were in the position to spoil her a little? Her parents were gone. He knew her brother and sister bred horses, which was no small job. Plus, Violet was on a honeymoon, and Kristy was four.

He was only too glad to step up.

Looking very contented, Rita grinned and opened her car door as he walked to his truck.

The high school was only a few minutes away from Old Town, in the opposite direction of the Co-Zee Inn, and he parked in back of the hotel in a spot next to Rita's.

Even from his truck window, he could see that Kristy had fallen asleep in her car seat.

Before Rita could fetch her, Conn got out of his truck and said, "I've got this. I don't like the idea of you having to carry her. How much does she weigh?"

"A lady never reveals that sort of information. But you're right—she's getting big."

After opening the door, he paused. Kristy's cheeks had two patches of pink on them, and her lashes were dark and long. In her velvet dress, she was a doll.

Would her brother or sister be just like her?

Conn's chest constricted as he undid the child's restraints, then lifted her out of her car seat. Without opening her eyes, she slumped against him, total dead weight, her head on his shoulder.

Rita was ahead of him, opening the back door to the hotel and ushering him up the carpeted stairs to the top floor. She opened the door and led him into a suite decorated in Victorian prints, the furniture velvet-upholstered, the wood gleaming and hand-worked.

She gestured toward the hallway, off of which a room waited, its thick curtains drawn, blocking the afternoon light.

After going inside first, she bent to turn on a night-light shaped like a round moon. It gave the room a hushed glow that whispered over a low bed covered by a flowered bedspread. Rita pulled back the covers as Conn kept holding Kristy, feeling needed for the first time since he could recall.

He finally laid the girl down, and she immediately turned onto her side, her hands tucked beneath her chin as Rita took off her Mary Jane shoes.

Conn had never put a kid to sleep. Or, more to the point, there wasn't a memory of it banked in his brain.

But that was okay, because there would be a bunch of opportunities with his own child in the future.

As he let the idea take root, he and Rita stood there, Kristy's even breathing marking the time, stretching it out until Rita finally took him by the shirtsleeve and brought him out of the room.

She quietly shut the door behind them, and they walked down the hall. When they reached her kitchen—a modernized room that was no bigger or more ornate than it needed to be—he finally spoke.

"That was nice," he said.

"Nice?" She had been just about to open the fridge. Then, after a second passed, she smiled, finally pulling the door toward her. "Sometimes I forget that it's little moments like the one you just saw that make everything else pale in comparison."

"Everything else?"

"You can guess what I'm talking about." She took out a package of tortillas, lettuce, tomatoes, green onions and cheese. "It'll be easy to forget about the angelic scene you just witnessed the next time Kristy refuses to clean her room or pouts like a pro when she can't have ice cream. But then the next time I put Kristy to bed, she'll seem so helpless and in need of me to watch over her that..."

Her back was to him as she stood at the counter, and she didn't make a move.

"That it makes all the hard times worthwhile," he said, hoping she wasn't teary-eyed.

"Yeah." Her voice was a wisp.

They didn't say anything as she seemed to regroup, going into the cupboard for a can of refried beans and a bottle of canola oil.

"I hope you like tostadas," she said, her voice definitely stronger now.

"Never turn them down. Can I help?"

"Are you handy in the kitchen?"

"Some would say so."

He doffed his hat, hanging it near the door on a rack, then went to the sink, where he washed up.

"Off your feet," he said, leading her to a chair by the counter.

She didn't complain a bit as he shredded lettuce,

chopped vegetables, cooked the tortillas and, soon enough, had dinner ready.

"Are you a table person?" Rita asked. "Or are you a fan of sitting in front of the TV while you eat?"

"TV all the way."

"Thank God." She headed toward the couch with her plate and a glass of water. "I try to teach Kristy manners, so we eat at the table. But in secret, I love sitting here and scarfing down my food. Besides, it's time for some football."

"A woman after my own heart."

The air seized up, as if he'd crossed a line. But it was true, wasn't it? Rita was his kind of woman, or else the old Conn would've never wanted a second night with her.

But had that been because the sex had blown him away or because of something more? Something that he was just beginning to discover?

She used the remote to turn on the TV to an NFL game. "Too bad it's not Longhorns game day. I never went to college, but I've kind of adopted them."

They sat, and he made sure he wasn't too close to her, but certainly not too far.

He put down his plate, plus the soda can he'd snatched from the fridge. "I went to Texas A&M, so it looks like we might have a divided household."

This time, she didn't seem to freak out about the reference to their future, and to Conn, that was good progress.

But even with that, he knew he still had a long way to go with Rita.

Chapter Eight

During the game, Rita had needed to sneak out and see to a few small matters in the hotel.

Conn hadn't seemed to mind, though, even if he'd made her sit down and rest afterward, bringing her some herbal tea from the kitchen and cleaning the dishes they'd used. Meanwhile, he'd also helped with Kristy when she'd woken up from her nap. He'd sat at the table with her and Rita as the little girl ate her tostada, and they'd chatted about Vi's wedding as well as all the things Kristy wanted to be when she grew up—a ballerina, a majorette and, this week, an inventor like Phineas and Ferb.

When they'd finally called it a night, he stood by the door. Kristy was in her room, drawing a picture for "Aunt Violet" for when she got back from her honeymoon.

"You know I'll be getting in touch with you again," he said quietly enough so that Kristy wouldn't hear.

Rita wasn't sure whether she should be encouraging Conn or saying a leave-no-doubt good-night to him. Her heart still told her one thing, her head another.

"In fact," he said, "how about you clear tomorrow night off your schedule? Get a sitter for Kristy, arrange not to work."

She didn't reveal that Monday was her usual night off. Still, as the owner, she was always on call. "What do you have in mind?"

Conn gave her that heart-spinning grin. "More talking, of course."

Right. He wanted to prove he could be reliable. And that was just how *she* wanted it.

Of course.

They'd said one of their awkward goodbyes again, with Rita avoiding temptation and closing the door behind him. And for the rest of the night, after she'd put Kristy to bed, then gone to her own big, empty one, she had slept restlessly.

Her mind was just too full of whats and hows: What was she going to do about Conn? How and when was she going to explain her relationship with him to Kristy?

She couldn't even quite define it herself at this point.

In the morning, the questions still hovered, but there wasn't much she could do about it as she manned the front desk and troubleshot for the few customers who were here during Thanksgiving week. She even called her sister, asking her to watch Kristy for a few hours tonight.

"Are you going out with that cowboy?" Kim asked over the phone.

Rita had told her that, yes, she was going out with the cowboy and she would tell Kim all about it later. She and her sister were close, but sometimes Kim, who would rather be hanging out on the ranch than fiddling around with a relationship, didn't quite get matters of the heart. Besides, Kim and Nick were leaving town on business tomorrow afternoon, so why start this up with her sister right now?

It could wait until after the holiday.

The day seemed to take forever to go by. One reason was that Rita was keeping her eye out for Conn, who had told her he would be checking in to her hotel today. But even with all her due diligence, she missed him when she took a break.

No matter, though, because once Rita was relieved at the front desk, she rushed up to the room and got ready to meet him. Kim had already gone to pick Kristy up from preschool and take her out for a meal at the Orbit Diner, so Rita was on time and in front of the hotel by the time Conn pulled his truck by the boardwalk.

She made her way into the car before he could get out to open her door.

Conn looked surprised at her efficiency, but he didn't comment on it. Then he gestured at a cluster of white bags waiting in a box between them on the seat.

"Do you mind making sure those don't spill all over the place?"

Dinner. The air was baked with the aroma.

"Stuffed potatoes?" she asked.

"Yup. They're from the market's food counter. I picked up a few other things they say a pregnant woman should be eating, too."

"Who's 'they'?"

"Online sites. I don't have a smartphone for nothing."

He'd done some research? The idea moved her in a way that most simple things didn't. It was just that he didn't have to take the time to do it, but he had.

Besides, Dr. Ambrose had advised her about eating healthy. Nice to know that Conn was going to help her with that.

He steered onto the street, and she asked, "So we're having a picnic?"

She'd worn a long red skirt with boots and a blouse, bringing a sweater for when the night cooled.

"It's not quite a picnic," he said. "I heard there's a drive-in about a mile away. You don't see many of those anymore, and the weather's still decent enough for us to go."

She sent him a slow glance. "You're taking me to the movies?"

Like…a date?

"They're playing good revival stuff, Rita. *When Harry Met Sally…* is first, then *Sleepless in Seattle.*"

"Chick flicks?" She laughed. "You really are out to impress me with your sensitive side."

"I wouldn't say it's *sensitive.* But I thought you might like a break from work with some comfort food and films."

As they drove, she wondered if she had accidently told him during some one-night-stand pillow talk about how *When Harry Met Sally…* was one of her favorite holiday movies, even though there were merely a few festive scenes in it. But Harry and Sally finally got together at the end, during a climactic New Year's party, and nothing made her happier in any film.

Nah, she wouldn't have told him that. Conn Flannigan was just that good at knowing what she wanted. And she couldn't stop remembering that he'd probably been that good with other women, too.

The truck tires crunched over gravel as they drew up to the ticket booth. He paid the admission fee, then drove past the concession stand and children's playground, finding a prime spot in the middle of the spread and cutting the engine.

Flicking on the radio, he accessed the sound system on low volume, providing pop songs to go with the advertisements for local businesses on the wide screen— the Queen of Hearts Saloon, Derry's Drug Store, the upcoming first-annual Cowboy Festival in March. Then he parceled out the food.

"You did do your research," Rita said as he set out the big baked potatoes stuffed with broccoli, then a salad, trail mix and apples swimming in a cinnamon sauce.

"I told you—I aim to give you the Pregnancy Comfort Experience." He motioned in back of the seat. "If you need blankets, I've got those, too."

Wow. Either he was truly this thoughtful or he was putting on one heck of a show for her. But she hated that her cynicism was rearing its ugly head, so she told herself to stow it away, just for a night. He had more than earned a chance.

As they were digging into dinner with their plastic spoons, a car with a young couple pulled into a spot in the row ahead of them. Through their rear window, Rita could see their silhouettes as they kissed.

She turned away, wishing her life could've been that easy with Conn.

But…wishing? She needed more reality, not fanciful thoughts.

"This is wonderful," she said. "I haven't been to a movie in…months."

"That's because you're always running around. When do you think you're going to get some rest?"

She dug into the potato, cheese stringing from her fork. "Are you about to lecture me?"

Yet didn't he have that right, as the father of their baby?

"I'm not the type to lecture anyone," Conn said, picking a bottle of water out of the box. "But I do want what's best for y'all."

She ate her bite of potato, then shook her head. "I never did take kindly to being watched over, you know. When people like Margery Wilmore at the hotel and other folks in town stick their noses into my business, it rubs me the wrong way. Sorry if I sound prickly with you."

"Prickly is part of your charm, Rita." He smiled, took a drink of water, put down the bottle. "And I don't say that in a cruel way."

"I'm not sure you have it in you to be cruel."

He looked just as surprised as she did. Had she meant it? Because, before now, she'd believed that Conn was a low-down, no good jerk for four long months. Yet the man who'd come back to her, hat in hand, wasn't anything like that.

What *was* the reality?

And which version should she count on?

"I hope," he finally said, "that I don't have it in me."

She left her food alone. "What if all of your memories are slow in coming back? I've read about amnesiacs never regaining their memories, and it's hard for them and their families."

"Right." He rested a hand on the steering wheel. "But all I can do at this point is make the most of what I've got, and that includes the baby."

It hit her hard, right then and there, that Conn had lost just about everything, but what he had now, he was going to treasure.

His other hand was resting on the seat, and as the pre-show concession-stand cartoons played on the big screen, she put her fingers over his own. Affection flashed through her, but it had nothing to do with a memory of that night between them.

It was all about what was happening now.

He looked down at his hand, her hand.

"Things would be a hell of a lot simpler if we could just start over," he said.

She bit her lip, then found the courage to answer. "Maybe we can try. A blank slate might do us a lot of good."

It was as if she had been wanting to say it forever, and now that it was out there, she breathed easier.

He seemed content, too. "Kristy mentioned yesterday that your family's going to be out of town for Thanksgiving. I'd like it if you'd come to our ranch, meet everyone."

The oxygen gushed out of her lungs. *Too soon,* she thought at first.

But as Violet had pointed out before, Rita and Conn were attached now. A child was going to be a part of both of their lives, and sooner or later, she was going to meet the family, if she and Conn wanted to provide their child with a happy, no-stress life. Hell, if Conn had really wanted to make everything tough, he could have just insisted on getting a DNA test and laid claim to their baby that way—then the child could *really* meet the Flannigan family.

Why not get along the best they could?

He added, "If you wear bulky clothes, we won't even have to tell them the news yet."

"You haven't said anything to them?"

"No. My brother Emmet pretty much knows we got together that night, but I haven't told him the rest. Nobody else knows much of anything. So there's no pressure for you. And I think Kristy would have fun with my three nephews. It'd be a good day all around."

She'd been resigned to helping Margery Wilmore serve turkey dinner to the employees who'd volunteered, with the benefit of time-and-a-half pay, to work on Thanksgiving at the hotel. She'd been feeling like a bump on a log, as it was, so...

No contest.

"Yes," she said. "We'd love to be there."

He broke into a smile, and it was so powerful that Rita squeezed his hand under hers.

The movie started—the chords of a piano and a bass playing over the speakers—and Conn's smile faded, his grip tightening on Rita's hand.

She knew he was thinking of kissing her, and she got that same impulsive urge that he always kindled in her to respond just as ardently.

Why not? it asked. *Be happy for once.*

"Rita," he said, and it was almost a question, but not quite.

Any way about it, an answer was all too easy. Without thinking, she surged forward, pressing her mouth to his, her hand sliding behind his head, her fingers burrowing into his thick hair.

It was more than a brush of lips this time—it was an explosion that shook her foundations, all her doubts sifting downward to tickle every throbbing cell.

He pulled her closer until she faintly heard the sound of bags and cardboard box crunching between them. Something—food?—hit the floorboards, but she didn't care.

Not right now, while he was kissing her so thoroughly, so deeply that a moan gathered in her chest, rising until the sound seemed to fill her.

So good, she thought. *So right...*

After wiping the food and containers aside, Conn swept her halfway onto his lap, kissing the tips of her mouth, the line of her jaw, the pulsing vein in her throat. Rita leaned back her head, reveling in every beat of stretched, passing time. The world around her blurred— a smudged picture of the movie on the screen, the fogging windows—but everything also seemed clearer than ever.

How could she ever think this was wrong?

One of his hands had traveled to the small of her back, and with the rashness of a teenager, she grasped it, brought it to her breast, which felt so sensitive that she almost wanted to cry out.

But she only sucked in a tight breath because she was also feeling tight between her legs—achy, needful.

Conn was the only one who could make that go away, she thought. Only Conn.

His thumb sketched her nipple, making it go stiff. She wanted his mouth there, too.

She pressed her lips against his ear, knocking off his hat in the process. "Conn," she whispered fervently.

That seemed to send a lance of need through him, and he shifted in an effort to bring her even closer to him.

At the same time, he hit the horn, and the sound chopped through the night.

In a flood of consciousness, Rita came up through the swampy state of her mind, breaking through to the surface of reality.

Her and Conn, in his truck, making out…

She wasn't sure how it had come to this, but when he touched her belly, as if in another question, everything that had gotten her to this point zoomed back.

Kevin had kissed her like this once… Kevin had left her, just as Conn once had…

She slid off Conn's lap, raising a hand to her hair, as if it were the most important thing ever for her to make it neat and tidy again. It had slipped from her barrette in a frenzy of curls, and that's not how she'd intended for it to be at the beginning of the night.

It needed to be kept back, controlled.

As if knowing that anything he said would be the wrong thing, Conn kept silent, settling into his seat to watch the movie.

Even as Rita tried like hell to get herself back together, she thought she saw a slight smile on his mouth. Instinctively, she almost smiled, too, until she realized that it was the last thing she should be doing.

Slowly but surely, Conn thought as he walked by Rita's side to his family's front door a few days later on Thanksgiving.

At the drive-in, he'd believed that matters with Rita were going straight to hell after that kiss. Their casual night had gotten a little out of hand. He hadn't intended to put any moves on her, but much to his shock, she was the one who'd started kissing *him*.

And he couldn't have been happier, because day by day, he was surer than ever that he had fallen for Rita on the night they had first met. She had been the one woman who could settle him down, and he had wanted to come back to her for more.

Yup, progress was being made, even if she had kept telling him over the phone these past few days that she was busy with the hotel and had no time for more drive-in movies or meals.

But she was here with him now, on his family's ranch, wasn't she?

So was Kristy, and she scrambled up the steps to the door before either Conn or Rita could get there.

"Beat you!" she said, her curls held back by pink ribbons that matched her skirt set.

"We're not far behind," Rita said. She had followed his advice and donned a light, loose black sweater that ended well past her hips, plus a gray cotton skirt. Both hid her baby bump, although the outfit was probably too warm for the sunny day. Her hair was pulled back in a loose ponytail, pinned by a silver clip, and he wondered when she would let down her curls with him again.

His stomach tightened, just at the notion.

Conn waited for Rita to climb the steps ahead of him, then went to the door.

Kristy peered in one of the long, beveled glass side windows, curious as a monkey.

"Now don't let my nephews roughhouse with you," he said to her before he opened the door to go inside.

She gave him a saucy glance. "I'm tough. Tommy

Griffin tripped me at school once and he didn't even hurt me."

"Tommy did what?" Rita asked.

Kristy made an exaggerated shrug. "I'm tough."

Conn stifled a chuckle, then looked at Rita. She was biting her lip, too, to keep from laughing out loud.

He bent and gave Kristy a tiny chuck under the chin. "You're as tough as your mom, aren't you?"

Rita said, "It's in the genes."

With a wink at Kristy, then a smile at her mom, he opened the door, indicating that the ladies should go in first. He heard Rita take a deep breath as she walked on by.

"No pressure," he said quietly.

She grinned, just as his mom came around the corner from the hallway.

"I thought I heard a ruckus!"

Conn greeted her with a hug and was just about to introduce Rita when Mom laid eyes on Kristy.

"Oh, my," she said, hand to her apron-covered heart. "Aren't you a sweetheart?"

Kristy, who seemed to be used to the praise, smiled and shuffled her Mary Janes.

"What's your name?" Mom asked.

"Kristy Niles."

"I could just eat you with a spoon!"

"Mom," Conn said. "This is her mother, Rita."

His mom came forward to give Rita a hug, but she didn't crush her bones as she tended to with her sons.

"We've heard a little about you, Rita," she said after she'd pulled back from their guest. "You're the reason Conn went back to St. Valentine."

"Conn stayed in my hotel," she said. "That's why he remembered me."

They had agreed on a cover story, and they would save the more colorful details for a later time, when she couldn't hide the pregnancy any longer. Of course, Conn had told Emmet not to leak the tawdry details of Conn spending a night with Rita to Mom and the rest of the family, and it looked as if Big Mouth had actually kept his word.

Conn added, "Rita and I became friends when I went to St. Valentine to investigate. She's been really helpful in trying to help me trigger memories there, and when I heard her family was out of town, I asked her and Kristy here."

"As you well should've." Mom's full cheeks were flushed, probably from the kitchen. But she looked sort of joyful, too, and Conn realized that Rita might've been the first woman he had *ever* brought home.

Hell, Mom might as well get used to it…and more with the baby on the way.

Mom linked arms with Rita and led Kristy toward the back of the spacious house, where everyone else would be. "We've got a playroom for the little ones. The twins and Jacob are already in there. I'm sure Kristy would love to meet them."

"When Conn told her about the littlest one, she couldn't stop talking about him the whole way here," Rita said. "She's good with younger children at the preschool."

The women chatted as Conn followed them down the hallway, with all its family photos on the walls. Apparently he had always been camera-shy, and Emmet had told him that he'd once gone through the collection and pulled all the pictures with him in them, hiding them somewhere on the ranch, much to Mom's ire.

Rita seemed to be surveying the walls for a peek at him, but she was out of luck.

They got to the playroom, which used to be Dad's ranch office until he'd passed on and Bradon had re-modeled a room in his own cabin and taken over desk duties. Now this airy space held a big plastic slide and playground set, plus toys scattered all over the carpet.

Ned and Nate looked up when Kristy entered while, in the corner, Jacob sat down hard on his butt, a plush turtle in hand.

Kristy headed straight for Jacob, who widened his eyes and smiled with drool-drenched enthusiasm at the sight of her.

In another corner, Conn's sisters-in-law had drinks in hand—wine for Trixie and lemonade for Hayley—as they sat in overstuffed chairs. The women greeted them from across the room, then fixed curious gazes on Rita.

Mom made introductions all around, and while she went to give hugs to her grandsons, Conn sidled up to Rita.

"Overwhelmed yet?"

"Not hardly."

"Because I already told you what comes next."

"Kitchen duty for you."

Although Mom had already let him know that Trixie and Hayley had brought a few side dishes from their own kitchens this year to give Conn a break, cooking most of the food was a job he usually took on with rel-ish. Or so they said.

"You go on ahead and take care of it," Rita said. "I'll hang out here and gab with the ladies. I'd like to watch and see how Kristy's doing before I leave her alone, anyway."

"You sure?"

"I'll be in the kitchen hovering over you before you know it."

She was so confident, and why not? The woman had been running a business since she was in her early twenties. She knew how to get along with people.

He didn't want to crowd her, so he went off to the kitchen, where everything he needed had already been laid out for him on the island in the middle of the bright, window-edged room.

The aroma of the turkey in the oven poked at a memory, but it didn't come to Conn just yet. It was weird how all the details seemed so striking to him, though: the copper rooster clock, the bluebonnet-print curtains, the iron pots hanging over the island.

On any other normal Thanksgiving, he would've been in here, merely taking time off from tagging and feeding calves and weighing bull calves, but not today.

Now he was wrangling a woman.

Every time he went to sleep these days, a little more of the brief affair with Rita would return to him. And every flash would fill him with a happiness that he knew he'd never felt before—an emotion that had *made* him want to stay, holding her, smelling her hair, getting every bit of her inside of him that he could.

Nobody had to tell him what the old Conn might've done in this situation he'd found himself in. But he *wasn't* the old Conn.

He wasn't even sure he liked him all that much.

Behind him, he heard movement, and he turned to find his mom entering.

"You feeling all right?" she asked, her Flannigan blue eyes tinted with concern.

Conn grinned, and the instant he did, he could tell that Mom was used to being assuaged by the gesture. Not convinced, necessarily, but consoled.

Picking up a potato peeler, he started to go at a sweet potato he'd already washed. The peels fell into the sink. "I'm feeling fine. Better and better, as a matter of fact."

Emmet's voice sounded from behind them. "Mom, you know that pot rustlers like Conn need their peace while they're cooking."

At the nickname for a chuck-wagon cook, Conn tossed his older brother a sarcastic glance, and Emmet grabbed a carrot stick from the island cutting board, munching on it and grinning. His brothers never let up on the teasing about his talent for cooking, calling him every quaint nickname from a biscuit shooter to a bean master. All Conn could say for sure was that he'd been comfortable in the kitchen when he'd come home from the hospital, his cooking skills intact even if parts of his brain weren't.

He went back to peeling. "I sense a varmint in the kitchen."

"Just grabbing some football snacks," Emmet said.

Mom said, "I want you to meet Rita. She's in the playroom."

"I've met her. Kind of."

"No, you didn't," Conn said.

"I'll do it at halftime." Emmet was already scramming. "Bradon and Dillon will come with me."

"No," Mom said. "They're greeting our guest now. They know how to be gentlemen, just as I raised you to be."

Mom went to the oven to check on the turkey. Meanwhile, Emmet had already moved on, muttering about missing even five minutes of the game, then pausing by a window to peer out of it.

There was something about the smell of turkey, something about the way Emmet was standing by the window that—

A flash came to Conn. *Emmet looking out a window in the family room, then smiling as a pair of headlights washed over him.* She's here, *he'd said, turning around to the rest of them. In his hand, he held a diamond ring as if it were the most fragile thing in the world.* Don't even hint to her about anything, got it?

He'd been uncharacteristically nervous, unbelievably excited about the woman he loved pulling into the driveway on another Thanksgiving, long before Conn had gotten in the accident and lost his memory....

Emmet saw the expression on Conn's face. "You look like you saw a ghost."

The smell of turkey, a diamond ring...

"I remembered you on another Thanksgiving," Conn said. "You had a ring and—"

Emmet held up a hand. "Yeah. The Great Thanksgiving Debacle. I was sort of hoping *everyone* would ultimately forget that year."

Although Emmet looked relieved that another piece of Conn's past had clicked into place, he also seemed a little heartbroken. Then again, the impression was gone before Conn could even be sure.

Emmet shrugged. "Sarah Humphries. Senior year in college, visiting me on her way to her own family's Thanksgiving. To make a long story short, she said no." He nodded in the direction of the front porch, where there was a swing that would be perfect for a marriage proposal. "'We're too young,' she said, and she was right. It's no big deal, though."

But as Emmet took up a bowl of chips and left the room, Conn wasn't so sure.

Even worse, he felt like half a person, because he didn't remember this seemingly big event in Emmet's life. Actually, he was just getting to know this brother—and the others—all over again.

Someday he was going to sit Emmet down for a beer and he was going to ask him about Sarah Humphries, not because it might jar a memory, but because he just wanted to be a brother again.

Would things ever be the same, though? Or would he always be experiencing his family's lives—and his own—through secondhand stories?

He continued peeling that potato, watching the skin fall away, as scattered as all his lost memories.

Chapter Nine

It hadn't taken long for Conn's sisters-in-law to invite Rita to sit with them in the playroom. Instead of Trixie's wine or Hayley's lemonade, Rita opted for a bottle of water from a minifridge near the window that overlooked an expansive lawn that seemed to disappear into a sea of windblown green.

"So Conn brought a girl home," said Trixie, who was married to Conn's oldest—and biggest—brother, Bradon. She had long, wavy deep red hair and clover-green eyes with a sprinkle of freckles over her pale skin.

Hayley, Dillon's wife, handed Rita her water as she sat down, her short, light blond hair brushing her jawline. "You have to understand what a remarkable occasion this is."

"He's told me all about his playboy days," Rita said. "But that doesn't matter much to me. We're just friends."

The other women traded "uh-huh" glances.

"No, really." Rita unscrewed the top of her water bottle. "I think he took pity on me and Kristy because we were going to spend Thanksgiving by ourselves."

Hayley took a long look at Rita's water, then her stomach. She put her own glass of lemonade on the low table in front of them, smiling almost secretively.

Feeling somehow discovered, Rita pulled her sweater away from her tummy. Had Hayley seen a telltale bulge?

Just then, Jacob started yelling at one of the twins.

"What's going on, Jake?" Hayley asked.

"Toy-tulle!"

The older boy gave the stuffed turtle back to Jacob and said he was sorry to his aunt, then his cousin. Kristy, like a little mommy, protectively led the two-year-old away from the bigger kids and back toward a pile of plush animals, where she and her new charge had been playing Zoo.

"Got to love kid drama," Trixie said, sipping her wine.

"Best entertainment ever," Hayley added.

Rita lost track of time, failing to check in with Conn while he was cooking, because Trixie and Hayley wanted to mom-talk about the highs and lows of raising children—subjects such as the true value of using time-outs as punishment and what sort of preschools were the right kind.

When Conn came into the room, Rita looked at her wristwatch. "Are you done already?"

"Yup. My dishes didn't take all that long and now Mom is herding the guys away from the games on TV and to the table."

"Let me get this straight," Rita said. "You gave up football to cook."

Conn shrugged. "The first game was a dud, but I won't miss the second."

He was so easygoing about it. Nothing much ever seemed to faze him, although his life was full of bumps.

He snuck over to where Ned and Nate were taking apart an oversize train like curious engineers, surprising them with tweaks to their ears.

"Hey!" both of them said, giggling.

Rita watched as Uncle Conn easily slid into the groove of playing with his nephews. Kristy, like a bee to honey, wandered over with Jacob, towing him by the hand next to Conn.

As she listened to him talking about how trains used to carry people all over the United States in the good old days, Kristy laid a hand on his shoulder, so naturally that it tugged at Rita's heart.

Her girl liked having Conn around. Had Kristy been deprived of having a man to guide her and love her just because Rita had been so adamant about being, as Conn said, "Wonder Woman"?

Rita thought she felt a stirring in her tummy, as if their baby was telling her that she wanted Conn around as much as Kristy did.

While Conn laughed with the kids, Rita thought about how he would react when he found out that they were having a girl together. Part of her wanted to tell him right now, just so she could see the gleam in his eyes that had been there on the night she'd confirmed that this was his child. But part of her...

Too soon, she thought again.

But when would the right time get here?

Conn's mom appeared in the doorway. "Dinner's up!" she said, taking off that cheeky Goddess of the Hearth apron she'd been wearing.

"Let's grab it." Conn picked up tiny Jacob, tucking him under his arm as the boy kicked his stumpy legs and belly-laughed.

The sound made the women laugh, too, as they followed everyone out the door, to a restroom where they washed up, and then to the dining room.

There, a long table waited, covered with an orange-and-brown plaid cloth, gold-trimmed china, sparkling silverware and a festive assortment of ribbon-strewn pinecones as a centerpiece. One chair at the head of the table had a gray cowboy hat hanging off the top of it.

"My dad's seat," Conn said, leading Rita to a chair, pulling it out so she could sit. "He had a heart attack and passed on about ten years ago, but we keep it open for him."

"That's a nice tradition." The patch of skin where he had rested his hand was even now tingling.

Conn was still carrying Jacob in one arm, and he went to put him at the kids' table, which was similarly decorated but with paper plates and plastic utensils. Kristy had already claimed a spot next to her adopted little boy, spreading out her dress over her lap like a lady.

Then Conn sat down next to Rita. When everyone was ready, Bradon brought out the carved turkey to applause. Then Conn's mom led a short prayer before they dug in to the turkey, an oven brisket with barbecue sauce, tamale-and-green-chile-corn-bread dressing, plus the mashed sweet potatoes, roasted vegetables and cranberry-orange salad that Conn had made.

All the while, Rita felt right at home, listening to the jokes they'd probably told to each other for years, hearing stories about Conn when he was young and carefree, collecting cars and shining them up for resale... but not before he'd taken them for a drag race or two on the back-country roads.

At the end of it all, when they were happily complaining about how full they were, Conn's mom sighed, glancing at the empty seat next to her at the head of the table.

"Even if years have gone by," she said, "I still can't help feeling as if he's going to stroll right through the door, apologizing for being late and then laying into the food without another thought to manners."

Conn lowered his head. How many memories did he have of his dad? Whatever he still retained, Rita got the feeling that it wasn't enough, and she wished she could help him with his amnesia more than she had done.

It was obvious that Dillon wanted to cheer everyone up, because his voice took on some spirit when he said, "I wish Dad was here now, too—for a different reason."

He shared a loving glance with Hayley. With her light blond hair, she looked like a Christmas angel that belonged on top of a tree.

Dillon put his arm around his wife. "We're having another baby."

The room erupted with congratulations and laughter, Conn and all of his brothers getting up to pat Dillon on the shoulders, Bradon's twins hopping up and down in front of a clapping Jacob, Conn's mom starting to cry with the good news.

When Conn gave Dillon a bear hug, Rita realized that Conn was present for *this* memory, at least. But when Dillon slid his hand over Hayley's belly, a sharp ache attacked her as she locked gazes with Conn.

They had news, too.

But he merely grinned, as if telling her that their time would come.

Was it actually too soon for him, too, in spite of all his determination to show her how responsible he really was?

Rita noticed that Kristy was sleepy-eyed in her chair, and that Jacob had come to lean against her, as if he was ready for Nap Land, as well. It was as good an excuse as any for her to leave the room, where the talk of babies was still going strong at the adult table.

Rita whispered to Conn, "Is there someplace I can put Kristy down?"

"Sure."

He went to Kristy, scooping her into his arms. Carrying her, which had begun to tax Rita, seemed so easy for him, as if her daughter didn't weigh any more than a feather. Besides that, putting Kristy to sleep was becoming somewhat of a habit.

God, she was going to have to talk with Kristy soon about just what Conn was to them, wasn't she?

Kristy's eyes bolted open, and she made a puckered face at Rita, who followed Conn out of the dining room.

"I'm not tired!" she said.

With that tone of voice, Kristy only proved how tired she actually *was*. "I'm sure Jacob's going to have a nap, too, Kristy."

"Ned and Nate won't."

Conn tugged on one of her curls. "The twins are going to have quiet time. You're not going to miss a second of play with anyone."

"Can I have a story?" Kristy asked.

"I think I could dredge one up." Conn arched an eyebrow at Rita.

Stories, she thought, smiling at him. She still couldn't get over how Conn might remember things like fairy tales when so many other tidbits would've been far more valuable.

They went into a guest room with a queen-size bed covered with a thick down patchwork quilt. Paintings of horses hung on the beige walls, and a lace doily decorated the end table.

After Conn put Kristy on the bed, Rita settled her in.

"Do you know 'Cinderella'?" Kristy asked Conn, who sat on the side of the mattress.

"Is that the one with the poison apple and the dwarves?" he teased.

Now that Kristy was lying down, her fight to stay awake was all but over, and she only murmured a faint "Uh-uh."

"All right," Conn said, softer now. "Does 'Cinderella' have a spinning wheel in it?"

"No." A whisper. Her eyes were halfway closed as she yawned.

Rita leaned against the wall, hugging herself, her head tilted as she listened to Conn launch into the story of a girl who worked all day and never went out of the house until life took a turn for the better.

That was what had happened to her, too. Conn hadn't been a curse. He'd been a good change. And it was looking more and more as if he could stay that way.

Couldn't he?

Kristy was slumbering before Conn even got to the part about the fairy godmother changing the pumpkin into a carriage. He carefully rose from the bed, pulling up the covers around Kristy a little more, then moving away.

Rita opened the door for him, closing it as they slipped into the dim hallway.

"I don't know what it is," she whispered. "But you've got the touch."

"I passed muster, did I?"

The comment had more weight to it than it would have under any other circumstances, and she swallowed, nodding.

"You're doing really well, Conn."

She was on the cusp of tears again—*thank you, hormones*—and her addled emotions didn't escape Conn. He used his index finger to angle up her chin.

"Hey," he said softly. "Why're you sad now?"

She might as well let it out. "Because I had everything planned. You were never going to show up again, and I was going to raise the baby by myself. It was a simple strategy."

"But then I ruined it all." His tone was light, yet that didn't mean he came off as uncaring.

And that made it even harder to talk.

"You didn't ruin anything. You just threw me for a curve, and I have no idea how to manage those nowadays. I'm fine when it's just me steering things along, but—"

He had bent toward her, shutting her up by pressing his lips to hers.

Her words dissipated under the sweet contact as she swayed toward him, her hands planted gently on his chest so she wouldn't sink to the floor.

He ended the kiss softly, stroking his thumb over her cheek and sending quivers through her.

"No matter what comes down the pike," he said, "I'm always going to be your man, Rita."

She allowed herself the luxury of believing him while she thought she felt the baby stirring once again, as if agreeing.

Pieces were finally falling into place for Conn.

Did it matter that they weren't the pieces he had initially set out to find in St. Valentine? No. These fragments he'd found in *himself* were what he suspected the old Conn had stumbled upon the night he had met Rita. And he guessed that what he'd found with her had ended the playboy's reign.

That night had obviously turned his life around altogether before he'd hit the road and forgotten most of who he was.

Even so, Conn thought the next night as he headed out of his room and toward the steps that led to the St. Valentine Hotel lobby, he wondered why uncovering his memories still seemed to matter so much when he liked how things were going now.

What was more important—who he had become or who he used to be? Did the memories make a man?

Something dark, like a stain that was growing, flexed in Conn, but he shoved it down inside of him as he descended the staircase and entered the lobby.

At first, Rita was the only person he saw in his heart-struck, myopic vision. She was the only person working the reception desk on a slow night.

Curly dark brown hair held back by a barrette, gray

eyes, full red lips, old-time hotel uniform, a smile that lit up his night…

Warmth flared through him, but then he took in his surroundings too.

She wasn't the only one here.

Kim, Rita's cowgirl sister, was standing by the desk. So was a brawny man Conn had briefly spotted at the wedding. He was a cowpoke, too, but he had an Iron Man-type beard, giving him a dark, dashing look.

Rita gave Conn a warning glance, though he wasn't sure what exactly he should be wary of.

Kristy bounded out from behind the desk, dressed in what looked to be a velveteen sweat set. She was holding a majorette's baton with Christmas-colored ribbons dangling from the ends.

"Mr. Conn!"

He got to a knee as she skidded to a stop in front of him. "You can call me Conn, you know."

"Okay. Aunt Kim and Uncle Nick are here."

And from the way Auntie and Uncle were eying Conn, he was sure that they'd come home from their business trip to finally have a word with him. As far as Conn could guess, Kim had said something to her brother about the rancher Rita was hanging out with, and based on the state of Rita's belly, they had done the rest of the math.

He rose to a stand, his pulse pattering like a rabbit's feet. Then he walked to the desk, extending his hand toward Rita's sister first.

"Hi again, Kim," he said. She took his hand in a strong grip, shaking it, making him think that she should meet his mom and create some kind of She-Woman club.

He offered the same gesture to Nick, who grudgingly took his hand while giving him the five-point inspection.

Rita was giving them both a lowered look. "They just stopped by to chat, Conn."

Chat sounded like a code word that actually translated into *interrogate*.

"I'm always up for that," Conn said.

Nick's voice was gruff. "We figured it'd be best to get to know you, seeing as Rita hasn't seen fit to do anything about that."

It couldn't be more obvious that Nick had taken the father-knows-best spot in the Niles family after their parents' deaths, and he'd never given it up.

"Conn! Conn!" Kristy was tugging on his shirttail.

He smiled down at her. She probably felt the tension in here, and like his nephews occasionally did when there was a disagreement in the household, she was trying her damnedest to erase it through a distraction.

"Watch," she said, spinning her baton.

After she finished, even stone-faced Nick gave her kudos, although he went right back to glowering at Conn a second later.

But someone, somewhere clearly thought Conn deserved a break, and Nick's cell phone dinged.

He exhaled while glancing at the screen. "Lady Guinevere is foaling, Kim. We need to go."

Kim was already moving. "See you later, Rita." Then she gave a brief nod to Conn before she went to Kristy and gave her a sound kiss on the cheek. "You can put on a show for us later, Kris, okay?"

"Okay," said the little girl as Nick came over to hug her, too.

She watched her aunt and uncle go, then slid an unreadable glance to Rita before going to a clear space in the middle of the lobby, where she started spinning her baton again.

"Careful," Rita said.

But Kristy was on a roll. "Conn! Watch!" She executed a little leap into the air, ending up in a *tah-dah* pose.

"Well done," he said.

She grinned and kept practicing.

Rita laughed, lowering her voice. "She's knocking herself out to impress you."

He'd noticed that Kristy had sort of latched onto him lately, and it made him smile. "She doesn't have to try hard."

Rita leaned on the wooden counter. "Sorry about Kim and Nick. She must've given him the rundown about us."

"He didn't look happy."

"Well, Kim doesn't know everything. I'd told both of them that I was pregnant back when I first found out, but I didn't say much about you. I've just been giving Kim bits and pieces, but I didn't sit them down for a good talk like I should've."

"Why did you put that off?"

Rita shook her head. "I don't know. Why do I put so many things off when it comes to this? Probably because I have no idea what to say. Kim's not very good at girl talk, and she would've asked all these very direct, protective questions I didn't want to hear. And Nick would've gone all Dear Daddy on me."

"They love you, that's all."

The *L* word just dangled there, but it was apparent that she wanted to leave it be.

Yet the longer it wavered in front of Conn, there for the taking, the cloudier his vision got, until...

Rita, lying in bed that morning, her necklace in his hand as he backed out of the room, closing the door as carefully as he could...

He shook himself out of the memory, which only added just the slightest bit more to the old one.

What did it all mean?

Rita gave a finger wave to Kristy across the room, then rested her chin on her hand. "I know Kim and Nick are disappointed that this happened again to me— another single mother situation. I guess I'm always going to be the girl who should've done better."

"No," Conn said, pulling out of his own thoughts and concentrating solely on her. On Rita, the only woman who mattered. "Don't do that to yourself."

"What—beat myself up about it?" A tiny laugh. "Welcome to my life."

"You've got to be kidding." He gestured around the room. "I'm not getting the sense that you're some kind of failure, Rita. Have you taken a good look at what you've gotten done?"

He meant more than running a recently prosperous hotel, too. He meant raising Kristy to be a great kid. He meant turning *him* around, a feat that no other woman had ever accomplished, as far as he could remember.

She paused, blushing, looking down at the desk with a smile. "I'm just so used to hearing the disappointment from other people. It's good to know that someone has noticed what I did right."

"I've noticed what was right from the very first."

They locked gazes. Conn almost lost his way in her eyes, but that was impossible, because she was the only clarity he had.

Is that why you can't stand the thought of being away from her? a little voice inside him asked. *Because she makes you believe you're one person when you used to be another? And you're scared to death that you still might be that guy?*

He would've dismissed that voice, too, if it hadn't sounded so much like the old Conn.

After Rita's shift was over, she, Kristy and Conn went up to her quarters with a couple of boxes of Christmas decorations that he was carrying.

"It's a weekend-after-Thanksgiving tradition," Rita had said downstairs, before she'd been relieved of work duties. Conn hadn't even made it out the door to run a few errands, as he said he'd been planning to, and Kristy had started talking about decorating and…

Here they were.

He put the boxes down on the sofa, looking toward the corner at the small tree in its stand. "You had time to go out and get this?"

"They actually deliver from the drugstore," Rita said. "Tomorrow, the employees will be trimming an even bigger tree in the lobby."

When he seemed dubious, she laughed. "St. Valentine is way ahead of the curve in some things. Derry Drugs has a deal with a tree farm not too far away."

Kristy piped up from her spot on the sofa. "Good customer service."

Both Conn and Rita gave her startled glances, then

laughed. The things her daughter picked up from everyday conversation.

"I think she's heard me talking about that a few times," Rita said.

Kristy rolled her eyes. "A lot of times, Mommy."

"Smart as a whip," Conn said, going over to Kristy and lifting her up so he could give her a twirl before setting her back down.

"Again!" Kristy said.

Conn obliged her with another go-round, and Rita remembered what he'd said in the lobby about her not being a failure—not with Kristy, not with anything. Who, besides Violet and *her* mom, ever really pointed that out to Rita? She'd never met a man who knew just what to say—and genuinely meant it.

But then, just as happiness was stealing up on her, a cold tide washed in. She couldn't shake the feeling that this was all so temporary...

"Hey," Conn said, taking her by the arm and guiding her toward the sofa. "Now's a good time for you to rest."

"Nap time for you," said Kristy, pulling a reindeer ornament out of a box.

Rita wasn't a bit tired. "You can't just—"

"Remember what I said about pampering?" He sat her down. "Don't be so stubborn about accepting a little bit of it. Do you have a small tub?"

"For what?"

"For soaking your feet. I read that it's a good thing for pregnant women to do."

As if the word *pregnant* had lured Kristy, she came over to Rita, getting on the sofa, resting her ear against Rita's tummy. Overcome, Rita stroked her daughter's hair, and when she glanced up, she saw that Conn was touched, too. He even seemed as if he would like to be the one trying to hear a heartbeat.

Then he came out of his haze. "The tub?" he asked.

Rita's throat hurt when she said, "In the hallway closet, top shelf."

Conn took one more moment to stand there, watching, then nodded and went to find the tub.

"Hi, baby," Kristy said as she lay against Rita. Then she raised her head. "What do we name her?"

She had already told Kristy to expect a sister, and the fact that Conn, the father, didn't know the sex yet grated against Rita's protective urges.

"I haven't thought of a name," Rita said.

"I like Ariel." Kristy lay back down.

Rita heard Conn's boot steps on the rug, and they slowed as he came back into the room. Had he heard what they were talking about?

If not, was now the time to tell him?

It seemed like such a momentous and private thing— the last brick in Rita's wall of defense against the hurt he could still cause.

But he was a daddy.

Rita sighed. If she was going to reveal something so meaningful, it couldn't be around Kristy. It would have to be one-on-one.

From the way Conn went about filling that tub with water in the bathroom and sprinkling it with some lavender-scented bath salts he'd found in the shower, Rita guessed that he hadn't heard anything about their child after all. It was a respite…and a burden, because she wanted it to be out there.

Finally.

But there would be a time, and for now, she reveled

in the feel of warm water bathing her bare feet while she watched Conn and Kristy hang ornaments on the tree—small dolls, paper stars Kristy had made last year, tinsel. Then, at the end, Conn lifted Kristy up so she could place a golden star on top.

Rita held her breath at the sight. She wouldn't have been able to do that for Kristy, but a man like Conn had the strength—and the desire—to lift her so high.

He and Kristy turned on the lights together, the glow of the tree illuminating their happy faces as he got to a knee and Kristy leaned against him.

This man could've been Kristy's father, Rita thought. If life were fair, he *would've* been, instead of Kevin.

Luckily, though, Rita would have a second chance at getting the father right with her new baby. This time, she was going to make sure this dad would do right by his child, as well as Kristy…

And maybe even by Rita herself.

Chapter Ten

The next day, Rita called her brother and sister to see if they were free to talk. There was no more putting it off, just as there was no more delaying the conversation Rita would need to have with Kristy.

It was time for Rita to make sure she did right by everyone, just as much as she was expecting Conn to do.

She took the afternoon off and drove Kristy over to the Crescent N Ranch, which Rita's bachelor uncle Rob had once owned and left to his nieces and nephew after he'd died. Rita, who'd never been much of a cowgirl, had opted for running the hotel while Kim and Nick had split duties on the ranch.

"We get to see the new horsey," Kristy said from her car seat in the back when they were about halfway to their destination.

"I'm sure Aunt Kim and Uncle Nick would love to show him to you."

"What's his name?"

Names again. Rita was still getting over Kristy's idea of naming the baby after *The Little Mermaid*. "You'll have to ask your aunt and uncle about that."

Rita kept driving, attempting to calm her nerves. She never looked forward to serious talks with her siblings, mostly because she didn't like to be questioned about her choices, and they were never shy about that.

As if it were a perfectly natural extension of the chat they had just been having, Kristy asked, "Is Conn going to be my daddy?"

Rita almost jumped out of her seat.

It looked as if this conversation wasn't going to wait until after she had finished the one with Nick and Kim.

She pulled over to the dirt shoulder of the country road, near an unhinged mailbox that had seen better days. Then she turned off the engine and peered around her seat so she could look at Kristy.

But what would she tell her daughter?

She decided to be as honest as she could. "Kristy, Conn is the daddy of the new baby, so he's going to be a really important part of our lives."

That was a start, but Rita didn't want to raise Kristy's hopes by saying he would be *her* father, too. She wouldn't speak for Conn, although there had been a growing hope, every time he interacted with her daughter, that Conn was the one man she could trust with hers, Kristy's and the baby's hearts.

But that was all it was right now—hope. Not a guarantee.

"I like Conn," Kristy said.

"I can see you do. He likes you an awful lot, as well."

"But he's not going to be my daddy?"

Why did Kristy have to be so darn dogged? "Sweetheart, I can't tell you what's going to happen in the future. I really wish I could. But I *can* tell you that I like Conn a lot, too."

Like? That seemed such a tame word for what she had come to feel for him.

Could it actually have turned into…love?

The notion made her pulse fly around in her chest, not knowing where to land.

Kristy got a goofy expression on her face. "You *like* him, Mommy?"

"Yes, Kristy." Rita could feel herself blushing. She couldn't believe that a four-year-old was razzing her. "I know you've never had to go through this before since I haven't brought a man into our lives. But I'm proud of the way you're handling it. It's made everything a little…different, hasn't it?"

Kristy seemed confused. Great.

"What I mean," Rita said, still avoiding those empty promises, "is that life isn't the same now with another person around so often. But you make Conn feel that he's welcome in our company. He appreciates that very much."

Kristy was fidgeting with the hem of her peach jersey shirt. "Lots of kids at school have daddies."

"And you want one, too. I know."

Rita rested her hand on Kristy's knee. She would do anything for her daughter, and she was just sorry that she couldn't have made Kristy's life easier than this.

But who was this harder for—Kristy or herself?

Kristy angled her head and gave Rita a sweet smile,

as if her mom were her entire world and she could never do anything wrong.

"Just remember," Rita said, touched, "there are so many people who already love you, and *that's* never going to change."

"People like you."

"Just like me. And if you ever have any more questions about Conn, or anything else for that matter, I don't want you to be afraid to ask. I'll always do my best to answer. Do you understand that?"

Kristy nodded.

Rita squeezed her knee. "That's my girl."

When she faced the steering wheel again, she had to take a moment.

That hadn't been so rough, had it? In fact, Rita felt a thousand times better.

Now it was time to see if her sister and brother were as sympathetic as Kristy.

After restarting the car and getting back on the road, they soon turned off into a graveled drive that led up to the Crescent N's main office.

Rita brought Kristy inside the brick building with gingerbread trim. The entry boasted an overstuffed couch with embroidered pillows, and Kristy hopped onto it as Rita called for her siblings.

From the back hallway came the sound of thumping boots on floorboards. Nick appeared, hatless and grizzled, followed by Kim, who looked as fresh as a sunny day. Kristy ran to them, saying hi.

Afterward, Nick jerked his chin toward the back of the building and said to Rita, "Tilly's in the lounge with some lunch for Kristy."

Time for that talk.

Kim held out her hand for her niece. "She's got peanut butter and jelly sandwiches without the crust, just how you like them."

With a backward wave to Rita, Kristy went with Kim to see the ranch's secretary as Nick walked into his office, which overlooked the stables in the distance. The room was utilitarian, just like Nick himself, complete with leather-upholstered furniture and a rugged oak desk that had belonged to Uncle Rob.

Rita chose a seat on the couch while Nick took to his desk chair. A few seconds later, Kim came in, shutting the door behind her.

"So you two want the skinny on what's going on with me," Rita said.

Nick had his arms crossed over his barrel chest as he reclined. "It'd be a refreshing change from being left in the dark."

Kim intervened. "I'm sure this isn't easy for Rita."

"It isn't." Rita rested her hand on a pillow, resisting the temptation to pull it on her lap and use it as a shield. "I've been overanalyzing everything to the point where I didn't know what was what. That's why I didn't want to talk to you. But…I'm ready now."

Hearing the words out loud jarred her.

Ready.

Ready for what exactly?

A burning outline traced the shape of her heart in her chest, telling her just what she truly might be ready for.

Conn, the surprise suitor who had gone more than the extra mile for her and the baby, and also for Kristy. It was as if Rita had gotten to know a new man these past couple of weeks, and she could barely match him up with the one-night stand who'd temporarily disappeared from her life.

Rita lifted her chin as she admitted everything to her siblings—and to herself. "I think I'm finally ready to move on with this man."

Conn was just wrapping up a few business calls with ranch vendors in his hotel room, making up for the time he'd lost because of the amnesia. Weirdly, he'd been able to get back into the swing of the physical ranch work, as if muscle memory had remained, but he hadn't remembered his business contacts and had been reacquainting himself with them during his recovery. He heard a knock on his door, but hadn't been expecting anyone. That didn't mean he couldn't hope it was the one person he was always longing to see, though.

When he found her at his doorstep, it felt as if his chest was being crushed—but in a good way.

Rita. And, as usual, she left him breathless, dizzy, nearly pushed to his knees for the wanting of her.

Maybe it was the way her cheeks were flushed, as if it was just as earth-moving for her to see him. Or maybe it was her hair, which was finally down from that barrette she usually wore, curling over her shoulders.

Just like on that memory-fogged first night with her.

He got a hold of himself, opening the door wider for her to come in. "Didn't expect to see you this early in the afternoon."

"I had some things to take care of and I finished before I thought I would," she said as she moved past him, leaving a trail of berries-and-vanilla scent. She smiled. "And they *are* taken care of."

"Are you gonna tell me what you're talking about?"

It was as if she had accomplished something she was intending to keep only to herself.

She leaned back against the wall. A few curls spread against the burgundy and deep pink velvet wallpaper.

"I had that talk with Kim and Nick," she said.

He almost asked, "What talk?" but he knew better.

"Did I get their stamp of approval?" he asked.

"Yeah. They're not ecstatic about the way we met, but they're my brother and sister, and I wouldn't expect them to be any less protective. They're going to stand by us, even if Nick grumbles about it every so often."

"Just so long as he doesn't bring out the shotgun and hunt me down. I got the impression he might be the type."

Rita raised her hands in a small shrug. "They were just angry that I didn't tell them about you sooner. They were hurt because they wanted to be privy to the situation. And, of course, they're worried that you're going to break my heart like…"

"Like Kevin did."

She expelled a soft breath, and when she looked up at him, her gaze was vulnerable. "I want so badly to let go of Kevin. I've been trying to do it for years, but I'm starting to realize how useless it is to go on just *trying* while not actually getting to the point where I've healed."

What had changed her? Was it too much to hope that it was him?

Her eyes seemed to tell him that he *was* the reason, and his blood surged.

"I had a talk with Kristy, too," she said. "She asked if you're going to be her daddy."

"Ah."

But, now that he really thought about it, why was that a surprise? Hadn't it been in the back of his mind since he'd returned here?

Hadn't it seemed so possible for the new Conn?

"I told her," Rita said, "that I couldn't make any promises for you. And I don't want to push you on this, Conn, but you should know what she's thinking."

"*I* was thinking that the baby and Kristy were a package deal." He touched one of her curls. Soft, silky. Damn, he could barely hold himself back because being around her, courting her, had been torture.

"Really?" she asked, her voice thick.

"Really." He traced a knuckle over her cheek. "Where is Kristy? I'll tell her that right now."

"She's with Kim and Nick. She likes to spend time at the ranch some weekends. You know how it is with girls and horses."

He trailed his fingers over her jawline, and Rita closed her eyes, biting her lip.

"When I said a package deal," he said, his tone gritty, "I was including you in that, too. I want more than a visitation agreement with the baby."

A slant of light seemed to rotate in the room. Or maybe that was just an optical illusion because, somewhere inside, he felt that his world had just been turned on its axis.

Or, at least, old Conn's world.

She opened her eyes. "I keep telling myself that this shouldn't scare me."

"What, being happy?" He laughed softly. "You just finished telling me that you want to leave Kevin behind."

"I do. But being scared… It started to become such

a part of me after what he did. And I always wanted everyone to think that I could deal with anything that came my way. That included you, Conn. I wanted to be strong, and I *didn't* want to put my heart out there for you to destroy. The same goes for Kristy and the baby."

"Don't be afraid, Rita. Not of me."

But maybe of the memories that might come back and change his whole point of view?

The thought was like a missile that had come racing out of the depth of his subconscious, where it had probably been firing up, ready to go at the slightest provocation.

He couldn't stand the notion of living the rest of his life like this, though, always on standby, always waiting for something to destroy the happiness he had found.

Like Rita, it was time for Conn to move forward—definitely, never looking behind.

She reached out to him, touching a button on his shirt. She was apparently still deciding to once and for all cross a line she'd drawn between them, a slash in the ground that looked so much like the wound that her ex-fiancé had gouged into her soul.

Then, something clicked in her gaze, a decision, and her gaze went glassy with oncoming tears.

Of happiness? Of sadness again?

"We're having a girl, Conn," she said.

He couldn't move for the longest second. Then, he finally asked, "A girl?"

"Yeah." She laughed, as if she still wasn't sure how he was going to take this.

But a jumble of girly names was already crowding his mind. Clarissa—that was his mom's name; maybe they could name their daughter after her? Or…what was Rita's mom's name? He thought that Abigail was a real nice one, too…

"A girl," he said softly, his heart melting.

He leaned forward to press a kiss to Rita's temple, to gather her into his arms as she sighed in what sounded like relief and, yes, happiness. As he buried his face in her hair, he couldn't imagine a time when he hadn't been filled with her, with the news that they were going to be parents of a beautiful little girl.

She clung to him, her cheek against his chest. He could feel wetness, her tears, on his shirt.

"Why're you crying?" he asked, stroking her hair.

"Because this turned out so much better than I'd ever dreamed it could."

Bowled over that he had the power to affect her this much—even when he felt as if he didn't have a lot of control in his own life—he kissed her on the bridge of her nose, her salt-tinged cheeks, then…

Then suddenly they were kissing for real, deeply, fiercely, as if they'd never kissed before.

She parted her lips, letting him in, and he explored her, languorously, with all the time in the world at their feet, her tongue meeting his as she started to slip down the wall.

Gently pulling her back up, he wrapped her in his arms, her baby bump brushing against him.

Rita started to fumble with the buttons of his shirt, and they came up for air, just as his nether regions started to push at his zipper.

"Is this a good idea?" he asked on the edge of a breath. "You're—"

"Going to have a baby, I know. You said you wanted

to pamper me, and I can't think of a better way now that we've got everything out in the open."

This wasn't what he'd had in mind, though. He'd been thinking more along the lines of waiting on her as she lounged on a couch.

"So pamper me," she whispered urgently, bringing him down for another kiss.

She'd gotten his shirt undone, and the air skittered over the bare skin of his chest. When she slid her hands up his ribs, he sucked in a stiff breath.

And when she circled his nipples with her thumbs...

He was truly a goner.

Yet that didn't mean he didn't still want to coddle *her*.

He took her long sweater by the hem, whisked it upward until it was over her head and on the floor. She was wearing a satin bra, her breasts bulging over the cups of it.

In a flash, he realized that she was bigger than the last time he'd seen her without her clothes on, but the memory fell to misty pieces, leaving only the present.

Lowering his mouth, he kissed the round firmness of her breasts, slipping his hands to her back so he could unhook the bra. When she was free, she raised her hands above her head, bending her elbows and resting back against the wall.

"Kiss me again," she whispered.

And he did, laving his tongue around her dark pink nipples until they peaked. Then, skimming downward in a path of lazy kisses, he pressed his mouth against her upper stomach.

Then her belly.

He paused, panting, using his hands to tenderly cup her there.

She pushed her elastic-banded skirt down so that the baby bump rode over it.

"Can you hear the heartbeat?" she asked.

Resting his head against her tummy, he listened for a pulse, but he wasn't sure if the pounding he heard was his own flailing rhythms or Rita's...or their baby girl's.

He stayed there for what seemed like forever, Rita stroking his hair, running her fingers over his temple, as if she were playing every chord that was singing in him.

No matter what the circumstances of this child's conception were, he knew that *he*—the new Conn—and Rita had made this little girl together. The old Conn couldn't ever interfere with what he was feeling now.

Nothing—not even memories that might change his perception of who he'd been or who he was—could ever take this away from him.

But even as he told himself that, there was a quiver in his head, as if something was beginning to come loose.

Rita whispered from above him. "Conn...?"

He glanced up at her, resting his hands on her hips. Without a word, he tugged down her skirt all the way, then her undies.

Her lips parted as she leaned her head back against the wall.

When she was fully bared to him, he took a moment to drink her in. His curvy, gorgeous Rita.

His. Not anyone else's.

He urged her legs apart, and she raised her hands

above her head again, her eyelids half-closed, her lashes like dark fans casting crescent shadows on her cheeks.

A chemical explosion—one part lust, one part a feeling he'd never known before—blasted through him, and he rubbed his cheek against her thigh. The scratch of his five-o'clock shadow seemed to dominate every other sound, even her heavy breathing.

Even the avalanche that seemed to be shifting in his head...

Furiously pushing everything in his mind away, he kissed his way up the inside of her leg, reaching up with a hand, touching her between the juncture of her thighs.

She inhaled, long and hard. "Oh."

He parted her folds, then kissed her there, as she slowly sank down the wall. He had to bring her gently to the ground as her moans came faster, rising into mewling cries.

Using his mouth to love her more, more, he brought her to a climax, and he'd never heard a sound so wonderful.

Not even in the memories he did have.

Between breaths, she said, "Did that...bring anything back to you?"

She was worried about the return of the playboy.

Conn tenderly rested a hand on her belly. "I'm in the here and now, Rita, nowhere else."

And it was true, because his mind had quieted, especially when she smiled, then reached for his gaping shirt.

He let her take it off him, and when it was pooled on the floor, he eased his hands under her, lifting her and carrying her to the bedroom.

After he laid her out on the bed, he hesitated, brushing his gaze down her once again.

But this memory he was making with her was stronger than anything he'd ever experienced before. He felt that, more than ever, he *was* this new man.

And he would always be.

"It's okay," she said to him. "We can do this while I'm pregnant."

That wasn't why he'd been just standing here, but he didn't tell her that.

In answer, he shucked off the rest of his clothes, then climbed into bed. She was watching him as if this were their first time.

But it actually was, wasn't it?

She took him in hand, caressing him, making him even harder than before.

"At this rate," he said, "I'm not going to last long, Rita."

"I won't, either."

They wouldn't need a condom—she was already pregnant, and the doctor had cleared him of any health issues during a checkup. He assured her of that as they lay on their sides, and she put her leg over his.

When he slid into her, flesh to flesh, he was suddenly blinded by a light in his head. He cradled her as they moved together, slick and slow, their cadence intensifying as the heat flared between them.

A blank slate, he thought, because that was what his mind was right now. Yet, thrust by thrust, he was starting to fill up with utter sensation: the smell of her skin, the sound of her rising gasps, the feel of her as they fit together so perfectly in this moment.

She was his everything, and he was hers, as his mind

brimmed with patchwork colors and images of Rita—her in that bridesmaid's dress at Heartbreak Hill, her at the drive-in with her lips lush and ripe from his kisses, her face as he looked into it now, seeing how deeply she felt for him.

Each picture was building, rising, new memories shooting and rumbling toward the sky...

As his body tightened, the images began to quake, as if they were going to come apart, and he fought to keep that from happening.

But then, instead of bursting into pieces, the images began to burn at the edges, consuming him, turning into a tower of light...

Seething, crackling, flexing—

With a breath of fire, the images *did* explode, sending jagged pieces in the air. But then, as they got closer to hitting the ground, they looked more like laces of ash, floating, drifting, landing on each other again like a scrapbook coming back together.

Conn held Rita, breathing hard, afraid to let go. Because there was something about those pictures that were darkening in his mind, triggered by the great emotion Rita had brought out in him.

Nothing else could've done this, he thought. But why did it have to be now?

Rita cuddled into him, her face burrowed in his neck. "This is true happiness," she said.

Swallowing, he refused to let her go, even as the pictures in his mind became clear again, turning into frames in a memory, just like a film reel.

He tried to battle the sight of it, but slowly, undisputedly, the reel started to play, and he saw what he had been fearing the most.

* * *

Conn opened his eyes, sunlight peeking through the curtains of a hotel room.

Slowly, he absorbed the sights around him: old-fashioned furniture like an armoire and a dressing screen, velvet on the walls and chairs...

Then last night came back, and he looked down at the woman next to him in bed who was still sleeping.

Her name was Rita.

Conn propped himself up on an elbow, tempted to kiss her awake, but something told him to wait. He wanted to look at her a bit longer because there had been something different about this woman, much more than any other one he'd ever bedded.

He'd flirted with her in a saloon, seduced her, been invited up to this room, and he had intended to leave in the middle of the night, yet... He hadn't.

He'd stayed long beyond his normal comfort level with a one-night stand. Hell, he was a real pro when it came to knowing when enough was enough, and he could scram with the best of them before things got serious.

But this time he had stayed, and he had lost track of time and common sense.

He touched her hair. Curls. They'd felt good against his skin as she'd trailed kisses down his body. The sex had been amazing, and honestly, there'd been a few moments during the afterglows when he'd thought to himself that he wouldn't mind coming back tonight, after he'd finished with business.

Not knowing what to make of this strange morning-after emotion, Conn crept out of bed, quietly getting ready to leave the room before she woke up. Maybe he would check in to a room somewhere else, since he hadn't gone to a hotel before stopping by the saloon last night for dinner. It would allow him to shower and spruce up, because he sure didn't want to be wearing day-old clothes and stubble to a professional appointment.

But just as he stepped into his jeans and boots, Rita stretched awake, the morning sun kissing her bare skin. She opened her eyes and smiled lazily when she saw him.

Then her gaze darkened when she realized he was getting dressed.

He knew just how to manage this. "Morning. How'd you sleep?"

"I barely did." She kept watching him cautiously.

On the floor, on top of her clothing, a necklace gleamed. Its pendant was an R that spread apart. He'd taken it off her last night, before they'd fallen into bed and never gotten out of it.

Now he bent to the ground and took it in hand, dangling it. "We dropped this."

She blushed.

He grinned, knowing the gesture was the best tool in his bachelor kit. "I thought you might let me take it with me today."

"Why?"

"Because I don't want to be anywhere but here, Rita, and if I have it handy, it might give me some consolation."

That seemed to please her, and oddly, her smile pleased him, too.

Then again, the entire night had been out of his realm of experience. He had genuinely listened to her

talking about her daughter. He had even found him-
self telling Rita things he usually didn't say to other
women—about his misspent time in college, about his
family. And that seemed to sway her now into trust-
ing him.

Thing was, he wanted to take this necklace with him.
In fact, he really did want to spend more time with her,
no lies there.

Just one more night, *he thought.* What would be the
harm?

"So what do you say?" he asked. "It's just some insurance—a guarantee I'll come strolling through the
lobby again tonight."

She paused.

He added, "I will *bring this bauble back to you."*

"Bauble? I spent hard-earned money on that. Not
much of it, but still…"

"I'll treasure it. I promise."

She laughed, and it was like a release for her. "As
long as you bring it back, Conn."

"I will."

And, damn it all if he didn't mean it with all his soul.

One more night, *he told himself again, even as he*
started to suspect that there was something else going
on here.

He went to the bed and kissed her, and that was when
his assurance totally evaporated.

Whatever it was that had gotten to him about her
last night had invaded him again, even as he still tried
to play it off. And now, with his lips pressed so affec-
tionately against hers, his body churned with a weak-
ness he didn't want or need.

He panicked, pulling back, recovering himself so

quickly that he almost fooled himself into thinking that it would be easy to drive away tomorrow morning, after he'd been with her one last time.

Rita, content as a kitten, sighed, then closed her eyes and went back to sleep.

Conn merely eased to the door, almost second-guessing himself and leaving the necklace on the end table. But he could fight this. He would come back tonight, and then that would be it.

Tomorrow, he would just write off this affair as a temporary infatuation and things would go back to normal again...

Chapter Eleven

What was wrong with Conn?

His arms had stiffened around Rita, and even though she hadn't been with more than two men her entire life, she knew that this wasn't normal for an afterglow.

A contented flow of hormones had been undulating through her, but now it cooled to a near stop. She rolled away from him a bit, enough to look into his eyes.

He was trying to hide whatever he was feeling; his gaze was shadowed, blocking her off.

Warily, she asked, "What's going on?"

He started to shake his head, but she stopped him by cupping his face.

"Don't," she said. Her worst fears pushed at her, conjuring questions, suspicions.

She didn't want to ask, but it was as if the words came all on their own.

"Did we just trigger something in your mind, Conn?"

He didn't seem to know what to say, and panic set into her. "I can see there's something going on. It's right there in your eyes."

Even as he rested his hand under her jaw, the shadows still loomed in his gaze. "Rita, I—"

She sat up, gathering the sheet so she could pull it over her chest. Suddenly, it felt as if he were more of a stranger to her than he had ever been. They should be in each other's arms after making love, not a million miles apart.

"What did you remember?" she asked and, God help her, but it sounded like another of her accusations.

He sat up, as well, bracing himself against the headboard, as if lying down left him too exposed. "It wasn't anything we have to talk about right now, Rita."

Now her heart was spinning, like a pinwheel caught in a stormy wind. "You're not going to tell me what you saw?"

He reached out a hand to her in what seemed to be a peace offering, but there was an edge to his voice when he spoke, indicating that everything *wasn't* so okay.

"This isn't the time."

"I think it is," she said.

When he blew out a ragged breath, she could see he was frustrated.

This couldn't be good, she thought. Why wouldn't he just tell her?

She wiped a hand over her face, but that was a mistake, because it blocked her view of Conn. And in that second of darkness, she saw another man in his place.

Kevin.

Conn couldn't have known it, but his refusal to be

honest with her was too damned reminiscent of her ex-fiancé on the night he'd sat her down at the kitchen table, telling her that he had been lying to her for a long time about loving her. He wasn't ready to be a father—he wouldn't *ever* be with her. And by the way, he'd been seeing another woman, who was waiting for him in a hotel just outside of town.

Lies. That was where the trouble started with men, because when lies were discovered, they led to full-on betrayal.

But was it fair to compare Conn to Kevin?

Why ask herself, when she couldn't even stop the comparisons?

She tried to still her pulse, but it was impossible. Yet she did manage to smooth out her voice.

"You're scaring me right now, Conn."

He cursed. She could tell that he felt trapped because, through and through, the Conn she had come to know was an honest man. Lying was eating at him.

The room was soundless except for her heartbeat nattering away in her ears, and when he finally started to talk, it was as if she was hearing him through a layer of cotton soaked by ether.

"You were right," he said. "Being with you did bring something back to me."

"What?"

He slowly connected to her gaze, his own still troubled. "The morning I left."

She paused, and relief pumped through her. "I thought you were going to say something worse. We know what happened that morning. You took my necklace, said you'd be back, then you got in that accident."

"That's what I remembered before now. But there's more to it than that."

More?

The word echoed like a growl in a dark cave.

He said, "Maybe my mind is playing tricks on me. Sometimes I don't even know what I *can* believe."

"Are you saying that your mind is creating false memories? Has that happened before?"

"No."

But he was wishing it had happened now, right?

"Just tell me," she said, because waiting was tearing her apart.

He stared straight ahead, and time ticked by.

Then he finally said, "It's like I don't even know the guy in the memory. I woke up in bed with you and—this is the only part that makes sense—I felt my heart grow about fifty times its normal size. You did something to me that no one else has ever done before, Rita."

That should be good news.... But then why did his low tone suggest that a bad part was yet to come?

Conn had pulled the sheets up and over his hips. "Emmet always tells me that I didn't invest much feeling in my one-night stands. And that was obvious in this memory. But I guess the fact that I felt something for you confused the hell out of me...." He emphatically shook his head. "No, I take that back. It confused the hell out of *him*."

No, you got it right the first time, Rita thought, fear gripping her again, even though she wanted so badly to banish it. *It confused the hell out of* you.

Because even if the new Conn was trying his hardest to separate himself from the old one, his memories were still a part of him. And once he got used to them being there again, how long would it take for him to go back to old habits?

How many other returned memories would it take for him to change back into who he really was?

Sheer horror was gripping her as the truth piled up on itself, making a bigger and bigger case for the reality of their situation—one she had been hoping would never, ever materialize.

"And what came next?" she asked in a monotone. Numbness. It was the only way she could hear the rest of this.

His skin had gone ruddy, as if he were mortified. "Just remember that I'm as far away from the old Conn as I can get. You can do that, right?"

She barely nodded.

He cautiously went on. "I remember how I wanted more time with you than just the one night we had together. I wasn't sure I even wanted to leave that morning, even though I had to. I was going to that appointment at the Hervy Ranch, and—this part isn't pretty, but I won't lie to you—I was trying not to wake you up as I got dressed."

She recalled that moment—her waking up, seeing him shrugging into his shirt, then grinning at her.

"You saw me in bed," she said, "and you picked up my necklace from the floor and told me you'd return it to me when you came back for another night."

"Yeah." His face got even redder.

She had a *really* bad feeling about this. "What is it, Conn?"

A thud of time slumped by before he said, "I was intending to be there only for one more night, and that's it."

Oh.

She wanted to yell at him for not sugar-coating the truth, for not letting her down easily. But she had wanted to hear it.

Anger and embarrassment forced the words out of her. "You just wanted a little bit more of the St. Valentine slut, and then you were going to gracefully let me down, just like you did with all the others."

"I wouldn't put it that way."

"Then what way *would* you put it?"

He merely shook his head, probably knowing that, for Rita, this was just like a slow-motion instant replay of a sick accident. This was confirmation that he hadn't planned to stick around at all, and in spite of all his recent good intentions, he would've eventually left the woman he'd so carelessly seduced, just as he had anyway on the night he was supposed to have shown up again at her hotel, and then the morning after when he still hadn't appeared, and then the day after that.

Even if he had come back for one more night initially, he would've dumped her in the end.

"Maybe," he said, "I would've changed my mind after I came back to you and stayed beyond that second night. We don't know that for sure."

"Don't even tell me you fell head over heels in love with me." A short laugh escaped her. "From what you just said, you don't seem the type who would've succumbed to that."

She started to climb out of bed, taking the sheet with her.

He grabbed the material, and she couldn't go anywhere—not unless she wanted to bare her body to him, and that would make her feel more stripped than ever.

"Rita, I'm *not* that guy. You have to believe me." He

sounded just as bewildered as she was. "I'm sure of who I am now. I'm ready to have children with you. And I'm not afraid to give my heart to someone—not after you came back into my life. Can't you see any of that?"

By now the shock had passed and churning hopelessness took its place, quivery and out of control.

"No, I can't see it," she said. "What I see is a man who's just on the edge of remembering other things about himself—things he probably won't like. What else did you do in the past that might affect us? What else will you recall that might make me feel as if I'm only a token chance at redemption for you?"

He sounded destroyed. "Why does it matter what I felt then? Because now I—"

"Don't say it." She couldn't hear a profession of love. She didn't even know what the word was anymore, didn't even know if old Conn or new Conn would be here a few weeks from now if more awful memories started rolling in, one after another.

Stubbornly, he finished his sentence. "I love you, Rita."

Dammit. She had been so ready to say it to *him* only minutes ago.

But now it was so easy to remember that Kevin, too, had said *I love you* to her. He was living proof that it didn't have to mean a thing.

A sob that she hadn't even noticed finally burst out of her. "You're in no shape to be telling anyone about loving them."

He reared back, because, once, she had told him he was unreliable. Certainly, he had proven otherwise, but with this surfaced memory, they were right back at square one.

"I'm a better man now than I was," he said, repeating what he had told her before, even though it didn't sound as if he quite believed it as much now.

She had to get out of here, because love was a trap. She'd been in it once, and she couldn't survive another epic failure—not when there was still enough time to save herself and her children.

"This is where it all begins," she said, hating herself for pointing this out. "You're going to start getting other memories back. Maybe you'll fall into old patterns, because people don't change as much as they'd like to think, Conn—they only do what's easiest for them. They leave their women because there's a newer upgrade to be had. They forget that they have responsibilities."

She could've been talking about Kevin...or the old Conn. Either way, neither could ever have a place in her life. She was sure of that now.

"This isn't about your ex," he said.

Yet even if that was true, the shadows still remained in Conn's gaze, telling her that her comments had struck home, and he was wondering if he could hold on to the personality he had adopted.

Since he had let go of the sheet, Rita cocooned it around herself now, leaning back against the wall for support as another sob gathered in her chest. Even with all this pain, she wanted to give him one more chance so badly.

Just one.

"Can you really tell me," she asked quietly, "if you're sure that you'll never go back to being the way you were?"

Something sliced through his gaze then, and she recognized it as pure doubt.

And that was all she needed to feed her fears, making them burn harder, obliterating everything else.

How had this happened? *Why?* God, it just wasn't fair that they'd been so close to happiness, only to have it yanked away like this.

But she'd known this day would come, hadn't she? And it made perfect sense that this memory would've resurfaced after the first time they'd been together, dredging up the same emotions.

She began to leave, only wanting to find her clothes and fumble her way back into them.

But his wrecked voice stopped her. "Rita?"

"Time," she murmured. Nothing made sense—not even her answer, until she pushed down that sob in her throat and her thoughts clarified slightly. "I need some time."

The longest pause in existence followed. Then he said, "I understand."

She tried with all her might not to look back at him, but damn her, she did it, and for the second time that day, she broke apart.

He was halfway out of bed, covered by the quilt he'd tugged over himself, his feet on the floor, his back hunched as he rested his arms on his thighs. It looked as if he hadn't slept in months, his gaze haunted, yearning, as he watched her.

Just as broken as she was.

Was this what the rest of their lives would be like together? One revelation after another that chipped at them, as well as their family?

She couldn't imagine subjecting Kristy or another child to that, not after one father had already left.

Couldn't imagine surviving it herself, either.

There wasn't anything more to say, so she went to the entryway, where her clothes waited in disarray.

Then she went out the door, feeling as if she'd left her heart in that room right along with Conn.

Conn packed up and headed home after that.

Why stay and make matters worse? Rita had told him that she needed some time, and if he was there looming over her, it would do more harm than good.

He'd written a short note to Kristy, leaving it at the reception desk for Rita, who wasn't on duty when he checked out. She could decide whether to give the message to the little girl he'd grown so fond of lately. It didn't say much—just that he needed to get back to his ranch and that he wasn't very far away and he would miss her.

But he didn't make promises to the girl. He didn't feel right about doing that anymore when he had no solid ground to base them on.

Would his memories change him?

Would he revert back to the old Conn one day and realize that he wasn't built for a relationship, then cause a lot of damage to the one he was in?

If Rita needed time to herself, then he probably did, too, so he drove to his family ranch, trying not to feel as if he was traveling back in time to the old Conn's house…and the old Conn's habits of escape.

The first night, he was able to keep to himself, without anyone bothering him after he'd let Bradon know he was back on the property.

The next day, he threw all his efforts into checking the fence lines, then had dinner in front of the droning TV by himself. He thought of how Rita liked to eat in front of the tube, too.

Actually, he couldn't get his mind *off* Rita.

Dammit, he felt as if there were an empty cave inside of him—one that had been lit up when he'd been around her and Kristy, but was now pitch dark.

The third day, he did some maintenance work in and around the cattle barn, managing to avoid any deep conversation with his brothers. But that night, Emmet showed up on Conn's porch with a six-pack of beer.

"You look in need of a drink," his older brother said.

Conn couldn't disagree, and he invited Emmet into his cabin. They plopped down on his couch, which was covered by a throw with spur decorations sewn into it.

Emmet popped open the caps on the two bottles, handing one over. "I've never seen you looking so hang-dog."

Conn's first instinct was to play the lone wolf and keep his problems to himself. But that was what the old Conn had done, and damn it all if he was going to fall into that guy's habits, no matter what Rita feared.

"I'm in a quandary," he said.

"It's your woman, isn't it?" Emmet flipped his hat off, and it landed on a nearby recliner.

"I wouldn't say she's my woman. Not anymore."

"I should've known right off the bat. You've been spending all your time with her, yet, suddenly, here you are again, looking like the saddest story in creation."

Conn put down his beer, untouched. "I got back a memory, and it told me that I intended to ditch Rita after I spent another night with her."

"You got some insight into your full libido, then. I'm sure it wasn't a surprise."

"Not after you told me over and over what I used to be like." He slumped in his seat. "It just showed me that I might really be as unstable for her as she thought in the first place."

"Why does that matter?"

Conn ran a hand through his hair. "She's carrying my baby, Emmet."

His brother gave a low whistle. "Congratulations?"

"I was happy about it, if you can believe it."

"With the way you've turned things around, I kind of do."

"Did I ever do that before?"

"Impregnate a woman? Not to my knowledge." Emmet narrowed his gaze at Conn. "And you never introduced the family to a woman before, either. Yet on Thanksgiving, you were here with a *real live* woman and her little girl."

Now that Conn had started sharing, it all came out. How he had wanted to prove to Rita that he was father material in spite of his shortcomings, how the memory had come back yesterday and thrown them both for a loop that might've ruined everything.

Emmet had been listening patiently, but when Conn was done, he asked, "I don't know what to say. My track record with women isn't exactly first-rate, either, so I'm not really one to come to for advice."

"Sarah Humphries?" Conn asked.

Emmet nodded, gripping his beer bottle. "I proposed to her on a whim. Generally, I tend not to think matters through to their fullest, and she knew that. And she was smart enough to say no to me." He exhaled. "I'm not sure where she is now, but I think of her sometimes. Wish I didn't, but I do."

The two of them sat there for a second or three, as if neither of them knew what to say about Conn's problem.

Finally, Emmet spoke. "I can't blame Rita for needing some time to herself to think. Put yourself in a woman's head for an instant. It's bad enough that they worry so much, but now, with what Rita knows about you, there's got to be a huge doubt about what other shenanigans you pulled."

"How could I fall back into my old patterns, though?" He shook his head. "You said once that there are a lot of people who would love a clean slate in life. I have that. So why do I think it's suddenly going to be cluttered with the decisions I made before now? Haven't I learned anything lately, and isn't that enough to overcome the old Conn?"

As he said it, he realized it was true. Rita, Kristy and the baby had altered him in a profound way. He'd grown up. He'd *owned* up to being the man they deserved.

But it really might take some time for Rita to see that. She'd said she was ready to get over what her ex-fiancé had done to her, yet Conn wasn't so sure that Kevin's actions weren't coloring everything that was happening now.

Emmet was nodding at Conn, drinking his beer, and smiling.

"What?" Conn asked.

"I like what I'm seeing. It'd be so simple for you to shut yourself away from all this trouble, yet here you are, ready to get back into the thick of it."

"Yeah, I am." He picked up his beer again. "Mom's

gonna burst when she finds out that Dillon isn't the only one who's having a baby."

"She always did have high hopes for you."

Rita had nursed them for Conn, too, and he wasn't going to disappoint her.

But how long would he have to wait until she gave him another chance to prove that?

As the sun brought morning to St. Valentine, Rita was already up and about, covering maid service for an employee who had called in sick, then taking Kristy to preschool and rushing back to the hotel to continue changing beds and tidying up.

She hadn't stopped working since Conn had regained that morning-after memory, and sometimes she wondered if this was her own way of blocking out the agony—by finding diversions.

Was that what she'd been doing the whole time since Kevin had worked her over?

While Rita pushed a maid's cart through the hallway, Margery Wilmore came up the stairs. She saw Rita and her hand flew to her ample chest.

"You're going to drive yourself into the ground," she said, going around to the other side of the cart and trying to pull it away from Rita. "Have you even eaten a decent breakfast? Pregnant women need more than the usual, you know. I heard you telling Janelle at the desk that you'd grab a big meal when you got back from taking Kristy to school."

"I had a little something." An apple and some yogurt sprinkled with granola. But she was still hungry, and she really would eat more just as soon as she was done with this room.

Margery was still on her. "I'm telling you, you should—"

"I'm fine." And she was. She would even have been able to handle all Kristy's questions about when Conn was coming back. Her daughter had listened as Rita read his note and Kristy hadn't stopped asking about him since.

But would Rita ever have any answers for Kristy— or herself? Especially with a man who might change before her very eyes?

When Rita grabbed a load of towels, Margery raised her hands in surrender. "At least let me help."

"I can do this myself, Margery." Just as she had raised Kristy and...

And would raise this baby?

As she entered the room and dropped the towels on the clean bathroom counter, she braced her hands on the edge, head down.

She was more exhausted than she remembered ever being. Her mind was always whirring with scenarios, even in the middle of the night. What if Conn decided that she wasn't enough for him, and he sought out another woman? What if he changed his mind about the baby and said he wasn't ready for one, after all?

She'd been blindsided by Kevin, but with Conn, she could be prepared.

Biting her lip to keep from letting her emotions take over, she bent her head.

I just want him to come back...

Margery was in the main room, changing the sheets, but Rita could still hear the woman's singsong voice.

"Where's that friend of yours? Conn? He was doing a good job of seeing that you took care of yourself."

Rita raised her head, looking in the mirror and seeing a total stranger with smudges under her eyes. Weird, because Conn had probably gone through the same thing a hundred times or more.

This was what it was like to not know yourself. But did that make *her* a bad person, unreliable?

Unsuitable?

"Conn had to go back to his ranch," Rita said. "But I thought you didn't like that I was taking some time off while he was around."

"I didn't say that."

Maybe her employee hadn't, in so many words. But Margery Wilmore was as transparent as a microscope lens.

"Anyway," Margery said, "maybe you should get him back here. He seemed to have an…attachment to you."

Rita rolled her eyes. She came close to blurting out that Conn was the father of this baby, that's why he had an attachment, but she couldn't. She didn't have the strength.

It would take a lot of it for her to admit that she did love Conn and that, in spite of what she'd said to him the other day, she did trust him.

But had she already pushed him so far away that he wouldn't come back? Would she be getting word from a lawyer sometime that he was going to go around her to get his parental rights?

Rita's head *kept* spinning with everything that was in it, but she pushed away from the counter, hanging the towels on the racks, then coming out of the bathroom.

Margery was halfway through making the bed. "Just look at you. I'll take over and—"

A wave of dizziness attacked Rita so fast that she

stumbled, the floor rushing up toward her. She grasped for something, but there was nothing to break her fall, and she dropped to the ground.

Right flat on her stomach.

The breath was knocked out of her, and she barely got out an "Oh, God."

Margery shrieked and tried to help her up.

"I'm calling Dr. Ambrose," Margery said through Rita's fog.

All she could think of was the baby and…

Wonder Woman. She'd been trying to do it all herself, attempting to forget about Conn, and now…

As she hugged her tummy, she touched Margery's leg.

"Conn," she said without thinking of the consequences. All she was doing was feeling, reeling, needing him here.

"Call Conn for me."

Chapter Twelve

Conn had been just outside St. Valentine, looking at a nearby ranch's cattle stock for sale, when he got the call from Margery Wilmore.

He dropped everything and was at the county hospital in record time, rushing into the waiting room and to the reception desk.

"Rita Niles?" he asked the nurse on duty. Around him, it seemed as if nothing else existed. There were just drab colors, dull walls and empty chairs, all stirred together and slipping down the edges of his perception.

The nurse asked, "Are you family?"

Yes, he wanted to yell.

Someone gently touched his arm, then led him away from the desk.

Kim, Rita's tomboy sister. She had her hat in her other hand, her gray-green eyes red-rimmed.

"How is she?" His question sounded like one slurred word.

"Rita's with the doctor right now. They're giving her an ultrasound."

The answer wasn't nearly enough. "Margery, the woman who called me, said Rita had fallen and she was holding her stomach afterward."

"Right. She got dizzy at the hotel and lost her balance. She wasn't in any pain, though. But she came right to the hospital, just in case."

Oh, God. Just in case.

Conn would never forgive himself for not being here if something went wrong. It was stupid to think he could've stopped this from happening, but he felt responsible anyway.

Maybe that was what all dads felt like.

Kim led him to the waiting area, but he stayed standing. Belatedly, he realized that Nick, Rita's brother, was also there, his own hat in hand as he stood by a magazine rack.

"Can you tell me about this dizziness?" Conn asked.

Nick wiped a hand over his mouth and trimmed beard. "Margery said that Rita was running all over the hotel, working, hardly taking time to rest properly. Rita thinks rules of nature don't apply to her or something. She's got to learn that she can't say no to what her body needs."

Did she only want to show everyone that she'd be all right on her own? Conn thought.

He came to a plastic chair, starting to take off his hat until he remembered that he had left it in the truck in his haste to get inside.

Slowly, he became more aware of his surroundings.

The sterile waiting room with its snack machines, the drab tile floor, the soothing pastel walls and the smell of strong cleaning products.

A hospital. And Rita was somewhere in here with their baby.

"I tried to get her to rest," Conn said. "But she's as stubborn as they come, and she's always so damned determined to do everything her way."

"From what I surmise," Nick said, "she could've been working off some demons that were riding her."

"Nick," Kim said. "Don't blame Conn for this. We know how Rita can be."

Conn stayed still. Kim was defending him?

She looked at him. "I'm not blind, and my hearing's pretty top-notch, too. I noticed how good you were for Rita and Kristy. Even Nick, here, has commented that Kristy is entirely devoted to you. And as for Rita? I haven't seen her this happy since Kristy was born."

What was she saying? That Conn was all right in their book?

Nick grunted, and—what do you know—it sounded a little like approval.

But Conn couldn't be sure, because the man restlessly moved toward a coffee machine.

At the mention of Kristy, Conn's thoughts revolved to her. Where was she in all this?

"Is Kristy okay?" he asked.

"She's still at school. Margery's going to pick her up when it lets out. It didn't make sense to scare her with the news about this."

"That's good," Conn said, and Kim slid an understanding glance at him, as if she could truly see that he wasn't some demented Lothario who'd come into town just to cause trouble with her sister.

Then she turned her attention to Nick as he took out his wallet to pay for a cup of coffee. Both siblings looked tired, as if merely waiting for news about their sister had exacted a toll.

Kim looked at Conn again, but she hesitated before she spoke. "You should know that you were the second call Rita wanted to make. The doctor was the first." She smiled wanly. "She asked Margery to contact you before even me or Nick."

The comment took a moment to soak in to Conn, giving Kim enough time to shrug.

"She trusts you that much," she said. "She wanted you here more than anyone else."

With a cosmic-size flash, everything came together for Conn then.

He saw life as it had been ever since he had made his way back to St. Valentine as a virtual stranger and been turned away by Rita at her hotel when he'd tried to give her necklace back to her.

He saw her baby bump as she rounded the reception desk that day. Saw her across the candlelit table at the fish shack, just after he had kissed her. Saw her giving him permission to touch her baby bump for the first time on Heartbreak Hill.

Then, most painfully of all, he saw her in bed the other day, looking up at him with such love in her eyes that he hadn't been able to fathom it.

Until now.

This memory flash had done it for him, made him feel completed. None of it enlightened him any more about his past, but it was the present that made him confident in knowing exactly who he was—the father of Rita's and his child. A man who could, beyond all doubts, handle being an instant dad to Kristy.

A man who loved Rita and couldn't live another day without her.

A door opened, and a middle-aged woman with her hair fixed into a bun came out, her doctor's coat flying open to reveal a set of pink scrubs.

"Dr. Ambrose?" Kim asked, taking Conn by the arm as they went to her.

Nick left his Styrofoam cup in the vending machine, where coffee splashed as it was poured.

The doctor was smiling. "Good news. Rita and the baby are just fine."

With a whoop, Nick wrapped Kim in a bear hug, and as Conn stood there, his knees just about giving out, they pulled him into their circle, too.

Emotion clogged Conn's throat as Nick patted him on the back and Kim squeezed his hand.

They were fine. Thank God.

Dr. Ambrose tucked her hands into her coat pockets, giving Conn a curious glance once the group hug had ended. It was as if she was wondering just who he was.

For the first time since he could really remember, he felt free in announcing his news to the world.

"I'm the father," he said, his voice cracking.

The doctor nodded, reaching out to touch his arm. "Well, you've got a baby who's healthy and doing very well, Dad. It's the mother who concerns me. She'll need to get some better rest and nutrition from now on."

Kim spoke up. "Conn will see to that."

He sent her a speechless glance. How quickly things changed.

Even Nick was smiling, but it was hidden pretty well by the shadow of his beard.

Dr. Ambrose gestured toward the doors. "You can see her now. She asked for the father specifically."

Rita had known Conn would be here?

From the way Nick and Kim looked at him, Conn guessed that perhaps Rita had only hoped that he would always be her man, even after all the ups and downs.

He was happy not to disappoint her.

He went with the doctor through the door and to a room off the hallway. When he saw Rita, she was reclining on an exam table, her white uniform blouse and dark skirt unbuttoned to reveal her rounded belly, which shone with what looked to be a gel smoothed over her skin.

But it was her eyes that Conn came to focus on—the glimmer in them as he entered the room.

"You came back," she whispered.

When he rushed to her, taking her tenderly in his arms, he whispered right back.

"Did you ever expect anything else?"

Even though Rita had worried that maybe she had blown it for good with Conn and he might not come back to her, deep in her soul, she had known he would be here.

Seeing him again sent her into a whirl of teary joy. She couldn't let go of him as they embraced, even when he pulled back far enough to brush the hair from her face and take a good look at her.

"Did you really have to put yourself in a hospital just to get me back here?" he asked.

Rita laughed anxiously. It was so much better than

crying. His return was like a dream, an assurance that they *would* be able to work through anything that came their way.

Real men never left for good, and Conn had proven that he was as real as they came, no matter who he was. How could she have ever doubted that?

He wiped a stray tear from her face. "The doctor told us that everything is okay."

"It is. I'm just feeling…" She rolled her eyes. "Jeez, these hormones, you know? They make me so weepy."

They smiled at each other, knowing it was more than just pregnancy wreaking havoc on her emotions.

He looked toward the entrance to the room, but Dr. Ambrose had left them alone, although the door remained cracked open.

Still holding Rita's hand, he took a seat by the side of the table. "You gave everyone a scare."

"It won't happen again. I promise." Yeah, look who was making the promises *now*. But she meant it.

"I'm going to hold you to that," he said.

His meaning was obvious—he was going to pamper her—and instead of resisting him, she welcomed the very idea.

Linking her fingers through his, she said, "I gave you about a thousand reasons to leave me, didn't I? But you persevered through each and every one of them, especially the other day. I said some things I regret, Conn."

"You said some things that were valid, too. There's no skipping over the fact that we still have a long road ahead of us, and there might be a bunch of potholes in it."

Empty holes. Places where his memories were still missing.

"Know what I've come to think?" Rita asked, her throat scratchy.

"What?"

"That if you haven't reverted back to being the old Conn already, it's not going to happen."

"Not with you in my life." Conn held her hand between the both of his.

To think, she had spent so much time avoiding men, probably because she had no idea how to live with one after being so thoroughly brokenhearted by her ex. Conn was willing to overlook that.

How had she gotten so lucky?

"For a while," he said, "I wondered if I had made you into some kind of fantasy that was stopping me from going back to being the old Conn. With you, I could act like someone else. But it wasn't true. I don't have to act." He rested his head against her hands. "You've made me over, Rita."

As she watched him, she cupped her hand over her belly. Conn had been reborn, she thought. A new life had been given to him just as much as he'd given life to their child.

He kissed her hand, and her heart warmed, slowly expanding until the tingling sensation flowed all through her.

"I love you so much, Conn," she said.

"And I love you, too."

Then he smiled, still holding her with one hand while he reached into a back jeans pocket with another.

When he pulled out her necklace, she marveled. "You held on to it?"

"It meant something to you, even if you didn't want to take it back from me."

She noticed that the *R* was in one piece, just like everything else.

He opened her hand, then put the necklace into it. First the pendant, then the chain, which spilled over the *R* like a sparkling gold fall of rain.

As the old Conn, he had told Rita that he would bring the necklace back when he returned for a second night with her. Now, it felt as if he truly had come back, against all odds.

And, this time, she accepted it.

There was nothing to say as she closed her fingers around the necklace. Nothing but sublime joy as he slid his other hand over her tummy.

"Your belly's slippery," he finally said.

"That's because of the gel Dr. Ambrose used for the sonogram. I told her she didn't have to wipe it off, because I was hoping you'd be here soon."

His blue eyes brightened as he got her meaning.

"I want you to see the baby," Rita said.

"I'll get the doctor."

Conn made short work of finding Dr. Ambrose; she hadn't gone too far from the room.

She entered, smiling. "I love this part," she said. "Excited parents are such a job perk."

After she turned on the machine and coated Rita's tummy with a bit more gel, she slid the transducer over the bump.

Rita didn't want to miss Conn's very first look, and he didn't disappoint. His face reminded her of how *she'd* felt when she'd first seen Kristy, and then this baby. Worshipful. Blessed.

His voice was raw as he took in the shape of their child. "She's beautiful."

Rita laughed. "She doesn't look much like either of us yet, does she?"

"I don't know." Conn leaned forward in his chair. "She has a stubbornness to her chin that seems awful familiar. She's got a lot of her mom in her."

Rita ran a hand down his arm. "And a lot of her dad."

When Dr. Ambrose let them hear the heartbeat, it pounded through the room, just like a symphony that was being composed pulse by pulse.

In the end, she gave them a picture of the child, then left the room again for what she said would be a short time.

"Look," Conn said, wearing his heart on his sleeve as he ran a finger over the photo. "I think she's waving."

Rita saw it, too, and as they stared at the picture, she knew that, no matter what the future held, this child— and Kristy—would always know just where their dad's heart was.

Nearly a week later, after Conn had moved back into the St. Valentine hotel, he brought the family on their first official outing together.

The H&H Ranch—which stood for Helping Hands, a charity that aided families who were down on their luck in St. Valentine—was having an open house. The endeavor had been the brainchild of Davis Jackson, but had become more of a project for the entire town, which had staffed the ranch with local talent that welcomed at-risk teens. The idea was to rehabilitate troubled youths here, through work and a connection with animals.

Conn carried Kristy into an area strewn with red-and-white-checked picnic tables and mistletoe center-pieces. The still-mild air was redolent with the aroma of barbecue. Next to them, Rita was carrying a small, wrapped "ranch-warming gift" for Violet and Davis.

Since Kristy had chosen the present, she asked, "Mommy, can I give it?"

"Sure." Rita handed her the beribboned box, which contained a collectible Precious Moments horse figurine to commemorate the spirit of the ranch.

"Yesss!" Kristy said, starting to climb out of Conn's arms.

He set her on the ground, but before she could run to Violet and Davis, who, along with Wiley Scott, were standing near a wagon filled with hay bales that would be rolling off for a tour of the property, she went to Rita.

"See you later, baby-gator," she said, touching her mom's tummy. Then she looked up at Rita with her big gray eyes.

"We're good. Don't worry," Rita said, winking at Kristy.

The girl smiled. After Rita's hospital trip, which they had tried to explain to Kristy without frightening her, Kristy had been extra watchful of Rita and the baby.

She waved, then took off, bearing her gift.

Conn put an arm around Rita's shoulders as they watched the little girl go. His hand brushed the chain of her *R* necklace, which she had started to wear again.

"Just what you always wanted," he said. "Another person who looms over you."

"I don't mind so much."

Rita leaned her head against him as, all around them, teens from every area of St. Valentine, whether they were miners' kids or from the east side of town, sat at the tables, eating barbecue and socializing. Country music played from the speakers, and a few teens had ventured out on the makeshift dance floor.

Violet and Davis had spotted Conn and Rita, and they waved, then walked toward them. Meanwhile, Kristy was tugging poor old Wiley Scott by the hand toward the stables.

When Violet arrived, she said, "Kristy's keen on the pony rides, and she enlisted Wiley to go with her."

"Looks like he's been pressed into service," Rita said as she hugged her friend.

Meanwhile, Davis and Conn shook hands.

"Recovered from those Scottish castles yet?" Conn asked him.

Davis, who was just as comfortable wearing designer suits as the faded jeans, flannel shirt and boots he sported now, shrugged. "They were cold and drafty. I missed it here."

"They were intellectually stimulating and historic," Violet said, nudging her husband. "But I was glad to get home. I'm only sorry I wasn't here for Rita."

"I already told you two that I'm okay." Rita rested her hands on the top of her belly. "The hospital trip was just a precaution."

Conn didn't say it, but that baby emergency was also a wake-up call. He hoped they never had one like it again.

Rita smiled up at him, and he pulled her closer.

Someone from the dance floor called to Davis.

"Duty awaits," he said just before he left, giving Rita a reassuring squeeze on the shoulder.

Violet's gaze trailed him, and the smile she wore told Conn that the honeymoon itself had been anything but cold and drafty.

"So," Rita said. "It's back to the grind, huh?"

"Hardly a grind. Don't get me wrong—I love a good honeymoon—but both Davis and I were chomping at the bit to get back. There's an estate sale coming up just outside of town and we always hit those in the hopes that there'll be something old and hidden that gives us more information about Tony Amati."

"You still haven't given up on that story?"

"Not while Jared Colton is hanging around town. Davis and I can't shake our reporter radar—there's something we haven't uncovered about Amati yet… and Jared."

Now *Violet* was being summoned by a volunteer who was running the hay rides.

"I've got to be a glutton for labor," she said, smiling. "See you later?"

"Always."

And she was off, leaving Conn alone with Rita.

The music played on, the kids on the dance floor clapping and having a good old time.

"I've been thinking," Conn said, watching them. "This place might need an extra cowboy on the volunteer staff."

"Really? Don't you already have your hands full enough on Shadow Creek?"

He was still doing business for the family ranch, but he hadn't told Rita everything yet.

"As I was saying…" He guided her to the left, where there was a view of the corrals and stables. Beyond those, a ridge of pine trees created a green horizon. "There's some land for sale out that way."

Rita looked up at him. "What about it?"

"Well, since those quarters of yours at the hotel are

getting a little crowded, I'm thinking of buying some acreage, making a home here in St. Valentine."

He had promised her that he was going to stay, forever and always, but he had been thinking of ways to show her his intentions in more concrete terms. The glistening sheen of her gaze told him that she didn't miss his message.

Tucking one of her loose curls behind her ear, he said, "I've been saving my money a long time, and this seems like a sound investment. What do you think of the idea?"

"I think I like it."

"I have another investment in mind, as well."

He didn't care that he was in a public place, amidst a hundred people. He didn't care who saw him, because his entire life was Rita and the kids now. Let the whole town witness the extent of his devotion.

From his pocket, he took out the ring he'd purchased the other day when he'd had business in Houston. He'd spent what had felt like hours picking out just the right one—a white-gold pave diamond in a swirl design. It was as complex yet as elegant as Rita herself.

She hauled in a breath when she saw it. "Conn..."

"I want to invest in you and Kristy, and...well, whatever we're gonna name our baby girl."

Bright-eyed, Rita locked gazes with him. "Kristy's still lobbying hard for the name 'Ariel.'"

He slid the ring onto her finger. He'd bought a bigger size than he thought she might need at the moment, knowing that she might be swelling up any day now. They could resize it later.

"I do like 'Ariel,'" he said. "I like anything you like."

Rita lifted her hand to see the ring glimmer in

the sunlight. Around them, it was as if everyone had stopped and held their collective breath, just as Conn was doing.

Before he could even officially ask her to marry him, she fell into his arms, whispering, "Yes, Conn, yes!"

He thought he heard applause, the sound of a hundred fragmented claps cheering them on, but to Conn, everything was in one piece.

His heart. Her heart.

And the beautiful, clear future before them.

* * * * *

Cherish™

ROMANCE TO MELT THE HEART EVERY TIME

My wish list for next month's titles...

In stores from 18th January 2013:

☐ The Heir's Proposal – Raye Morgan

& The Secret That Changed Everything – Lucy Gordon

☐ Mendoza's Miracle – Judy Duarte

& Fortune's Hero – Susan Crosby

In stores from 1st February 2013:

☐ The Texas Ranger's Reward – Rebecca Winters

& The Ranger's Secret – Rebecca Winters

☐ A Bride for the Maverick Millionaire – Marion Lennox

& The Billionaire's Fair Lady – Barbara Wallace

Available at WHSmith, Tesco, Asda, Eason, Amazon and Apple

Just can't wait?

0113/23

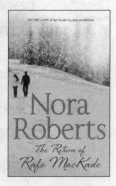

The World of Mills & Boon®

There's a Mills & Boon® series that's perfect for you. We publish ten series and, with new titles every month, you never have to wait long for your favourite to come along.

Blaze®

Scorching hot, sexy reads
4 new stories every month

By Request

Relive the romance with the best of the best
9 new stories every month

Cherish™

Romance to melt the heart every time
12 new stories every month

Desire™

Passionate and dramatic love stories
8 new stories every month

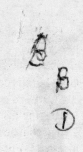